Penguin Books
Penguin Skills Series

Penguin Speaking Skills
Teacher's Book

Teacher's Book

Penguin
Speaking Skills

John Green
Mark Hilton

Penguin Books

Penguin Books Ltd, Harmondsworth, Middlesex, England
Viking Penguin Inc., 40 West 23rd Street, New York, New York 10010, U.S.A.
Penguin Books Australia Ltd, Ringwood, Victoria, Australia
Penguin Books Canada Ltd, 2801 John Street, Markham, Ontario, Canada L3R 1B4
Penguin Books (N.Z.) Ltd, 182–190 Wairau Road, Auckland 10, New Zealand

First published 1985

Copyright © John Green and Mark Hilton, 1985
All rights reserved

Typeset, printed and bound in Great Britain by
Hazell Watson & Viney Limited,
Member of the BPCC Group,
Aylesbury, Bucks

Set in VIP Palatino and Helvetica

Introduction

This Teacher's Book provides a key to the exercises of the Coursebook of Speaking Skills, with tapescripts of the cassette exercises and notes on intonation and appropriateness.

It will be seen that within the three-tier structure of the book each unit and each section follows the same basic form.

1 A brief introduction, for the student and the teacher, to the area of language to be reviewed. To be read and discussed.

2 A collection of **Model Exchanges** presenting examples of this language in the appropriate register. These exchanges are designed to be entertaining and thought provoking. The questions in the **Checkpoint** section which relate to these exchanges have been chosen to draw attention to specific functional or cultural peculiarities in the language reviewed, and to encourage the student to think about the reason behind the employment of specific forms in specific situations. Notes for guidance on these questions are provided.

   At this stage it is intended that the students should only read through the dialogues and discuss their socio-linguistic implications; they should not attempt to enact them.

   Recordings of the model exchanges are provided for repetition and practice only after the students have studied and discussed the language presented in the model phrases section, whilst the suggestions for role play in pairs or groups are intended to be used after the completion of the structured exercises, as revision and extension of the language encountered and absorbed.

3 A list of **Model Phrases** or sentences commonly employed in the communication of the function under review, with notes on specific uses when appropriate. Students should at this stage check their understanding of the lexis and structures in the material presented.

4 **Exercise 1** relates directly to the list of model phrases or sentences. Once again the student is invited to make his or her own judgment of the areas of usefulness of the language presented, which can and should be teacher monitored, before being asked to produce vocally the phrases themselves. We suggest a triple repetition of each phrase as a kind of ritual familiarisation with the kernel phrases, which should then be compared with the models provided on the cassette as they occur in the dialogues of the model exchanges. Where appropriate, students should be encouraged to complete the half-phrases or sentence introductions presented, with the teacher monitoring the appropriateness of these continuations. To facilitate this monitoring process we have included a recommendation that these continuations form the basis of a written exercise

supplementary to Exercise 1, which the teacher can collect and mark for accuracy and appropriateness before proceeding with Exercise 2. These monitored written exercises can then serve as the basis for further roleplay or discussion in pairs or groups when the unit has been completed (see below).

5 You will see that we regard it as imperative for the students to become familiar with the language presented in each unit intellectually, verbally (from the point of view of being able to produce the kernel phrases with acceptable intonation and stress), and as much as possible emotionally, *before* attempting to produce such language vocally and without direction. Each unit therefore contains, in **Exercise 2,** a text or graphic-based exercise or quiz to increase the student's confidence in his ability to differentiate between the implications of the different language forms within the given area of study. In this book-centred exercise the student is required to find or connect appropriate initiations and responses and either mark them in his or her book or note the answers in an exercise book or notepad. Although text-orientated, the variety of design and layout in these exercises should provide an agreeable and valuable springboard to the next exercise.

6 **Exercise 3** In the majority of units Exercise 3 requires the student to produce vocally the language options he or she has selected in Exercise 2. In most units, between eight and ten exchanges are provided. This number is sufficiently small to facilitate teacher monitoring of individual students while at the same time providing sufficient student practice at this stage. The teacher will have to become adept at stopping or pausing the cassette recorder to give students time to answer.

To conserve tape, only enough time to stop and start a standard recorder has been allowed before the tape continues with a suggested response, correctly spoken. Because some students may be using the book for self study, we preferred to have each suggested response (SR) follow immediately after the speaker to whom it relates, rather than having them all on a separate tape or at the end of each exercise.

We would emphasise that in such an area of vocal reproduction it is clearly impossible to give one right answer to the language puzzles we have posed. Our suggested responses are therefore based on a thorough knowledge of common and current British usage, but in certain cases variants will be admissable – although less so here than in Exercise 4 – and the teacher should monitor such variants carefully before rejecting them as unsuitable. The notes we provide will help you, as well as pointing to the essential intonation patterns required in specific forms – intonation patterns which can be compared against the SRs provided on cassette. Of course the tapescript provided for Exercise 3 should be used as a basis for deciding the appropriateness or correctness of the options chosen in Exercise 2, as well as providing a basis for study and/or repetition of Exercise 3. The exercise should be repeated if the student's answers are misconceived or if his or her intonation is wildly inaccurate.

7 **Exercise 4** is generally a free or semi-directed exercise which calls on both the student's imagination and assimilation of the language forms presented in the unit. Differences in responses and opinions should certainly be tolerated, within the parameters of the prescribed task, and a thorough testing of as many as possible of the kernel phrases reviewed in the unit is to be encouraged. The suggested responses which follow each prompt are to be taken as suggestions only (unless otherwise directed in the key) and are once again based on the instinctive responses of native English speakers. They can be of use as intonation pattern models and as an indication of the mood or tone of the response appropriate to the prompt, rather than as indications of the one and only right answer. In certain exercises the student is required to initiate an exchange, not to respond. In such cases his or her cue to speak has been given as a 'beep' signal. The tape should be stopped immediately after this beep to enable students to answer – before the suggested response is heard on tape.

8 **Exercise 5** asks the students to suggest variants to the phrases provided in the unit, and is intended to emphasise the fact that the phrases are examples only, and not comprehensive. The three-tier design of the course does present the possibility that language will be selected which more correctly belongs within the register/area of a different section of the same unit.

9 It should be emphasised again at this point that the design of the student's book is deliberately non-chronological. With the exception of Section A, Unit 1 on hesitation and time-giving techniques, which we advise students to study and practise before attempting any other unit, the subsequent units are as free-standing as they are interdependent, and the teacher should not feel constrained to proceed systematically through the thirty units provided. Wherever possible we have indicated points of cross-reference in the notes which follow, and it is our intention that the book and cassettes should be used, as the title implies, as practice materials for developing a neglected skill rather than as a traditional step by step course book. We hope that you – and your students – will find it useful.

John Green
Mark Hilton
London 1985.

Contents

Contents

Section A
English for
everyday situations

Unit 1 **Giving yourself time**

This unit on hesitating is necessarily a little different from the others in format; getting the student to make use of the techniques requires the exercises to be done without any pre-examination of the material.

Checkpoint

Notes for guidance

1a No, they don't.
 b They haven't. This means that Michael must approach his invitation appropriately.
 c Michael's hesitation gives him time to decide on his approach. You may find it necessary to discuss his approach, but the aim is to consider the hesitation.
 d Clearly not – she hesitates while thinking out her reply.
 e Students may say Michael is shy – we think not. He needs to decide on his invitation form, particularly in view of Linda's answer, which was perhaps unexpected.
 f Obviously Linda is unsure. She probably doesn't want to, but can be persuaded.
Roleplay/Pairwork   This dialogue could be the basis for practice in persuading and agreeing/disagreeing, when the appropriate units, particularly C7, have been covered. Continue the dialogue, Michael to persuade Linda to come.

2a No, he doesn't. Henry hesitates while consulting his diary/order book. It is most important to say something while doing this.
 b David wants it done at rather short notice, so a tactful approach must be worked out.
 c He probably can. *I think* gives a positive note.
Pairwork   Students should finish the exchange, with Henry agreeing to do it and David responding.

3a Simon is feeling guilty and needs to work out his answer.
 b Janet is annoyed – the intonation and attitude conveyed in this speech must reflect that.
 c Probably not. He might be going to say *Well, I think so . . . , but I'm not really sure . . .*
Pairwork/Roleplay   The last question invites the continuation of Simon's speech, so develop it into a full dialogue of ensuing argument. Use of sarcasm (Unit C10), persuading (Unit C7), and suggesting (Unit C9) with appropriate agreements and refusals would be needed.

Play the model exchanges on the cassette for the students to listen to. Students to repeat and practise; teacher monitors for intonation etc.

Exercise 1

These phrases are usually said with mid-level intonation. *Well, you see* and *Ah, that's a problem* should have a fall-rise.

Exercise 2

The answers can be read out as given, or short forms used. Students should be encouraged to use different pause-fillers rather than the same one each time.

Tapescript

1 How many days were there in February 1932? (*Pause*)
   Suggested response: Um . . . let me see . . . there were 29.
2 What is the deepest part of the sea in the whole world? (*Pause*)
   sr Er, let me have a look . . . it's the Mariana Trench, near the Philippines.
3 How long does the Sun's light take to reach the Earth? (*Pause*)
   sr Um . . . er . . . about eight minutes.
4 Which is the nearest star to our solar system? (*Pause*)
   sr Er . . . Proxima Centauri.
5 When did Columbus discover America? (*Pause*)
   sr Er . . . let me think . . . in 1492.
6 Which English king stepped to his death through a window? (*Pause*)
   sr Ah, that's a problem . . . it was King Charles I.
7 Where did the Great Fire of London start in 1666? (*Pause*)
   sr Um . . . let me see . . . it was in Pudding Lane.
8 Why is there a monument to Nelson in Trafalgar Square in London? (*Pause*)
   sr Oh, um . . . let me have a look . . . because he commanded the victorious English fleet at the Battle of Trafalgar.

Exercise 3

Tapescript

1 How many places are there where you can join the tour? (*Pause*)
   sr Um . . . there are four.
2 How many bridges does the tour cross? (*Pause*)
   sr Let me see . . . four bridges.
3 Which bridges does it pass without crossing? (*Pause*)
   sr Let me have a look . . . Chelsea Bridge, Vauxhall Bridge, Waterloo Bridge, Blackfriars Bridge and . . . er . . . one other one.
4 Where exactly can you join the tour in Trafalgar Square? (*Pause*)
   sr Let me have a look . . . oh, outside the National Gallery.
5 How many times a day can you join the tour in Trafalgar Square? (*Pause*)
   sr Um . . . eight times.

6 Where exactly can you join the tour near Victoria Station? (*Pause*)
sr Erm . . . let me see . . . in Grosvenor Gardens.
7 How many times a day does the tour leave from Piccadilly Circus? (*Pause*)
sr Er, let me have a look . . . er . . . twelve.
8 Does the tour leave more times a day from Westminster Abbey, or from Piccadilly Circus? (*Pause*)
sr Oh, er . . . let me see . . . from Piccadilly Circus.

Exercise 4

There are no suggested responses. Students should give their own.

Tapescript

1 How long is it since your last birthday?
2 What exactly were you doing this time last week?
3 How long is it before your next holiday?
4 What is your favourite food?
5 How long have you been working on this unit?
6 How many pages are there in this book?
7 Which country would you most like to visit?
8 How many questions have you answered in this unit?

Exercise 5

Ask students to suggest acceptable variants on phrases reviewed. Allow them to add acceptable variants to their books, unless they appear in Unit 1 of Section B or Section C.

Pairwork, groupwork and roleplay suggestions

Students will need to pause while working out their responses. The teacher should monitor students' use of appropriate hesitation devices.

Unit 2 **Encounters, greetings and goodbyes, introductions**

Checkpoint

Notes for guidance

1 This is informal, and used in a wide variety of everyday situations.

2 This is slightly more formal. The tone of the conversation suggests slightly older speakers, or a slightly more formal situation.

3 No, it's a little joke, made to hide social nervousness – a way of asking, *What has he told you about me?*

Roleplay Students could be asked to continue this exchange.

4 She's clearly a stranger. This is the first time she has met him. Also she called him Mr Wyatt, not Henry, so she could be either (a) younger, or (b) less senior than Henry Wyatt. Henry's reply is more relaxed than Davina's self-introduction. He is either (a) older, or (b) senior to Davina.

5 These two have obviously known each other for some time, but have not met recently. They could be (a) fellow students, or (b) fellow workers.

Roleplay Students could be asked to continue this exchange.

6 The point here is to show how often we use such intensifiers when we are (a) nervous, or (b) apologising to or thanking people. Particular attention should be drawn to intonation patterns when listening to the dialogue on cassette.

Play the model exchanges on the cassette for students to listen to. Students should repeat and practise. Monitor for intonation, etc.

Exercise 1

Supplementary written exercise Ask students to provide written continuations for each of the phrases and then practise saying them aloud. Monitor for tone, appropriateness and effect.

Exercise 2

Suggested answers are as in the tapescript for Exercise 3. Any deviant responses should be examined for differences in tone, appropriateness and effect.

Notes

1, 2 As in dialogue 5, the exchange assumes that the speakers are on familiar terms.

3 *How do you do?* Answer: *How do you do?* This exchange revises the universal pattern.

4 *Mrs Mackintosh? My name's Harper.* Answer: *Hello, pleased to meet you.*

If students choose, *How do you do?*, remind them that the first speaker would have to reply, *How do you do?*

5 *Brian, have you . . .?* etc. This is the exchange with three elements: *No, I haven't but I've heard a lot about her*, followed by, *Not all bad, I hope!* Explain the alternatives for Catherine, e.g. *Oh really, what have you heard?* or, *Oh dear! Who's been talking about me?* Point out that (weak) humour is used to hide nervousness at first meeting. Ask students to suggest alternative phrases.

6 The lateness of the hour prompts the exclamation, *Oh dear!* and an apology for leaving.

7 *Thanks for a really lovely meal.* Answer: *Not at all. It's been a pleasure.* Explain this standard reply to thanks. Students should think of other situations where it is usable. Go on to explain that no language formulae exist in English for the beginning of a meal. There is no way of saying, *Enjoy your meal*, etc. When absolutely necessary, English speakers will use the French *Bon appétit*.

8 *Hello! How are you?* Answer: *Fine, thanks. How are you?* Emphasise the importance of (a) the second speaker asking after the first speaker, and (b) the intonation and stress on *you*.

Exercise 3

Remember to pause the cassette recorder to give students time to respond.

Tapescript

1 Goodbye. (*Pause*)
  sr Goodbye. See you again soon.
2 Frank, how nice to see you again! (*Pause*)
  sr Hello, Peter! What have you been doing since we last met?
3 How do you do? (*Pause*)
  sr How do you do?
4 Mrs Mackintosh? My name's Harper. (*Pause*)
  sr Hello, pleased to meet you.
5 Brian, have you met Catherine? (*Pause*)
  sr No, I haven't, but I've heard a lot about her.
  sr Not all bad, I hope!
6 It's half-past eleven. (*Pause*)
  sr Oh dear! I'm terribly sorry, but I really must be going.
7 Thanks for a really lovely meal. (*Pause*)
  sr Not at all. It's been a pleasure.
8 Hello! How are you? (*Pause*)
  sr Fine, thanks. How are you?

Notes on the tapescript

1 Check low-rise on *soon*.
2 Check for rise on *Peter* to indicate surprise.

3 Ensure fall on second *How do you <u>do</u>?* It is not a genuine question.
4 Check that stress falls on *meet*.
5 Check for pause after *haven't*, and for lightness of tone – in the upper part of the vocal range.
6 Check for stress on *terrible* and *really*.
7 *It's been a pleasure* – Low pre-head, high-fall on *pleasure*.
8 Check for even stress on *Fine* and *thanks*, and nucleus high-fall on *you* at the end of the question.

Exercise 4

Remember to pause the cassette recorder to give students time to respond.

Tapescript

1 You want to introduce Simon to Mary. You're not sure if he knows her already. (*Beep*)
 sr Mary, have you met Simon?
2 Say hello to Sheila. She's an old friend from school who you haven't seen for a long time. (*Beep*)
 sr Hello, Sheila, how are you? I haven't seen you for ages.
3 Introduce yourself to Miss Todd. She might be able to help you with your studies. (*Beep*)
 sr Miss Todd? . . . Hello! My name's Carrington.
4 Answer Simon who meets you in the street:
 simon Hello! How are you? (*Beep*)
 sr Fine, thanks! How are you?
5 Say hello to your colleague, Susan, who <u>you</u> meet just after you've said hello to Simon. (*Beep*)
 sr Hello, Susan, how are you?
 susan Fine, thanks. How are you?
6 Say goodbye to your hostess, Mrs Taylor. It's half-past midnight and you have an exam in the morning. (*Beep*)
 sr I'm terribly sorry, but I really <u>must</u> be going. I've got an important exam tomorrow morning. Thanks for a lovely evening. Bye!
7 Your friends don't want you to leave, but you've got an appointment at 3 p.m. You <u>have</u> had a very nice lunch, though, and <u>they</u> have paid for it! Perhaps they'll take you out again one day. (*Beep*)
 sr I'm terribly sorry, but I've really got to go. I'm meeting someone at 3. Thanks for a really lovely meal – and see you again soon!
8 Catherine has bored you with stories of her family for fifteen minutes. Say goodbye to her politely but firmly. (*Beep*)
 sr Well, it was really nice talking to you, but I'm afraid I must be going. See you again soon.

Notes on the tapescript

1 No indication is given of situation. sr is neutral and normally acceptable.

2 Check for sincerity of *Hello* and emphasise stress on *ages*.

3 Check for hesitation on *Miss Todd?* Students should substitute their own names, of course. A possible alternative is: *May I introduce myself?* – but this is rather too formal here.

4 Check intonation against the tape. Further practice: students should repeat the exchange as if they are (a) bored, (b) angry, (c) tired, (d) in love.

5 Same as 4.

6 Explain the need to give a reason for leaving. Introduce *lovely* if necessary.

7 A long answer is required. Many variations are possible, but stress is needed here to convey four separate things: (a) the need to leave, (b) reason for leaving, (c) thanks, (d) hope for reunion.

8 Do not accept an abrupt or aggressive goodbye. Compare with . . . *really nice talking to you* on the tape. Ask students to think of other similar situations where such 'lies' are necessary.

Exercise 5

Ask students to suggest variants on the phrases reviewed. Allow them to add acceptable variants in their books, unless they appear in Unit 2 of Section B or Section C.

Pairwork, groupwork and roleplay suggestions

Refer back to the students' written continuations of the phrases in Exercise 1 (supplementary exercise). In the light of subsequent practice (Exercises 2, 3, 4, 5), ask them to use these monitored sentences as the basis for conversation in pairs or groups, extending or developing their original ideas.

Unit 3 **Information gathering**

Checkpoint

Notes for guidance

1a Betty and David are in a library rather than a bookshop; this is suggested by Betty's answer.
 b Betty is an assistant, David a reader.
 c *Could . . .* is appropriate, as Betty's job is to help readers.
 d David uses these patterns because he is asking Betty to go to the trouble of consulting the catalogue in the first place, and in the second place he is asking her to recommend another possible source.

2a Linda and Justin are in the street.
 b Linda is trying to find the insurance company. Justin is going somewhere.
 c This is used to get attention – not as an apology – by the British.
 d The use of *happen to* indicates that she merely needs some information, nothing more.
 e Justin is probably in a hurry and Linda needs to apologise for delaying him more.

3a On a bus. Janet has just got on.
 b Janet is a passenger. Jim is the conductor or perhaps another passenger.
 c *Can you tell me . . .?* because he can be expected to know. *Do you by any chance know . . .?* because he can't be expected to know.
 d Something like, *Do you happen to know where I can get the tube?*
Roleplay   This exchange can be continued, with Janet eliciting further information about the tube and Jim giving it: which line, number of stops, map of the Underground needed. They are near Marble Arch.

Play the model exchanges on the cassette for the students to listen to. Students to repeat and practise; teacher monitors for intonation, etc.

Exercise 1

All of these phrases and the indirect questions which follow should be uttered in the upper part of the voice range. Otherwise they sound surly and offensive.
Supplementary exercise   Get students to provide a written continuation of each phrase and then practise them aloud. Monitor for tone, appropriateness and effect.

19

Exercise 2

Suggested answers are in the tapescript for Exercise 3 below. Any deviant responses should be examined for differences in tone, appropriateness and effect.

Exercise 3

Remember to pause the cassette recorder to give students time to respond. Remember the intonation note to Exercise 1.

Tapescript

1 You are at the information desk at Euston Station in London. You want to know how long the Inter-City 125 to Glasgow takes. (*Pause*)
   SR Excuse me. Can you tell me how long the Inter-City 125 to Glasgow takes, please?
2 You have arrived outside a bank, but it is closed. Ask a young lady who is passing what time it opens. (*Pause*)
   SR I'm sorry to trouble you, but do you happen to know what time the bank opens?
3 You are in London and want to visit the Houses of Parliament, but don't know the way there. Ask a policeman. (*Pause*)
   SR Excuse me, officer. Could you tell me how to get to the Houses of Parliament, please?
4 You are at a bus stop and want to go to Marble Arch. There is a bus coming – is it the right one? Ask the old lady who is also standing at the stop. (*Pause*)
   SR Excuse me. Do you by any chance know if this bus goes to Marble Arch?
5 You are at a travel agent's. You want to know the cost of a seat on the British Airways shuttle to Edinburgh. (*Pause*)
   SR Excuse me, can you help me? Can you tell me how much a seat on the British Airways shuttle to Edinburgh costs, please?
6 Your watch has stopped. Ask a passer-by the time. (*Pause*)
   SR I'm sorry to trouble you, but do you happen to know the time?
7 Your car has just broken down. There is a traffic warden just up the street. Ask her the way to the nearest garage. (*Pause*)
   SR Excuse me. Could you tell me the way to the nearest garage?
8 You have decided you would like to play tennis. Ask someone if there are any tennis courts nearby. (*Pause*)
   SR Excuse me, can you help me? Do you by any chance know if there are any tennis courts near here?

Notes on the tapescript

1 You are speaking to an information clerk – use *can*.
2 You are speaking to a young woman passer-by – it's important to show that you only need some information and are not trying to 'pick her up', otherwise she might not respond.
3 Policemen and policewomen are there to help the public, but

command respect, hence, *Could you . . .?* Note term of address for a policeman or policewoman: 'officer'.

4 The old lady can't be expected to be familiar with every bus route and you only want some information.

5 It's part of the job of a travel agent, so use *can*.

6 It is especially important to ask this in the right way. Asking the time is a standard 'pick-up' technique in many languages.

7 Traffic wardens are like policemen and policewomen – they command respect, and you don't want her to give you a parking ticket while you are going for help! Use *could*.

8 You are talking to a stranger, and it is a rather unusual question to be asked suddenly.

Exercise 4

Remember the intonation note to Exercise 1.

Tapescript

1 You are in a bookshop. You want to find a book on English cooking. Ask the assistant for help. (*Pause*)
sᴿ Excuse me, can you help me? I'm trying to find a book on English cooking. Can you recommend one?

2 You are in a department store looking for a souvenir to take home. Ask another stranger, who is also looking, for his advice. (*Pause*)
sᴿ I'm sorry to trouble you. Do you happen to have any good ideas for souvenirs of London? I can't think of a thing.

3 You are in the street and need to find the Underground. Ask a passer-by for help. (*Pause*)
sᴿ Excuse me, can you help me? I need to find the Underground. Do you happen to know where the nearest station is, please?

4 You are in the Underground station at the ticket office. You don't know the right line for Piccadilly Circus. Ask the clerk. (*Pause*)
sᴿ Excuse me. Could you tell me which line to take for Piccadilly Circus?

5 You are on the Underground but you are not sure if it is the right train for Piccadilly Circus. Ask another passenger. (*Pause*)
sᴿ Excuse me. Do you by any chance know if this is the right train for Piccadilly Circus?

6 You are at the theatre box office. You want to know the time the performance starts. Ask the booking clerk. (*Pause*)
sᴿ Excuse me. Can you tell me what time the performance starts?

7 You are in your seat in the theatre and realise you haven't got a programme. Ask the person next to you where she got hers. (*Pause*)
sᴿ I'm sorry to trouble you. Could you tell me where you got your programme, please?

8 You want to send a telegram home. You are in a post office and want to know the cost. Ask the clerk. (*Pause*)
sᴿ Excuse me. Can you tell me how much it costs to send a telegram to Holland, please?

Notes on the tapescript

1 You are speaking to a shop assistant, so *can* is appropriate.
2 You are talking to stranger and only asking for advice, so use one of the last phrases in the list.
3 Again, you are talking to a passer-by. Only information is needed.
4 The clerk's job is to sell tickets, not to give information, so use *could*.
5 Again, you are asking a stranger.
6 This is part of the clerk's job, so use *can*.
7 Although you are asking a stranger, *Do you happen to know . . .?* and *Do you by any chance know . . .?* are inappropriate to this question, hence, *Could you tell . . .?*
8 This is part of a post office clerk's job, so use *can*.

Exercise 5

Ask students to suggest variants on the phrases reviewed. Allow them to add acceptable variants to their books, unless they appear in Unit 3 of Section B or Section C.

Pairwork, groupwork and roleplay suggestions

Situations

1 Asking a stranger (policeman) in the street for directions: how to get somewhere, means of getting there, and time needed.
2 Asking a railway/airline booking clerk about getting to somewhere: single and return journeys, times, prices, etc.
3 Asking a fellow student to recommend an activity for an afternoon: e.g. swimming, tennis, visiting a museum. Then find out where to go, how to get there, how much it costs, how long it takes, etc.

Unit 4 **Giving information and instructions**

Checkpoint

Notes for guidance

1a Shirley is taken aback – Jim's statement is too abrupt.
 b Fall + rise. *I beg your pardon!* Emphatic stress on *beg*.
 c Jim has been impolite and aggressive.

2a Linda needs to attract Frank's attention.
 b Linda wants to tell her superior something which is (i) out of context, and (ii) he might take as a criticism.

3a David uses the order of landmarks which she will pass on the way – geographical order.
 b Joanna signals that she has noted each landmark in turn. She is perhaps writing them down.
 c David emphasises the last landmark as a starting point for the next stage.
Roleplay   Continue the third conversation. Joanna repeats the instructions back to David, and David confirms that each stage is correct or puts right any mistakes. Joanna should do this from memory.

Play the model exchanges on the cassette for the students to listen to, repeat and practise. Monitor for intonation, etc.

Exercise 1

The first five phrases and the sentence that follows them should all be uttered in the upper part of the voice range.
Supplementary exercise   Get students to provide written continuations of each phrase and then practise saying each one aloud. Monitor for tone, appropriateness and effect.

Exercise 2

Suggested answers are as in the tapescript for Exercise 3 below. Any deviant responses should be examined for differences in tone, appropriateness and effect.

Exercise 3

Remember to pause the cassette recorder to give the students time to respond. Remember the intonation note to Exercise 1.

Tapescript

1 You are in a non-smoking compartment of the Underground, and you see a man starting to smoke a cigarette. (*Pause*)
  sr Excuse me. I hope you don't mind my saying so, but this is a non-smoking compartment.

2 You are at the bank. A lady in front of you is leaving. Her gloves are still on the counter. (*Pause*)
  sr I say, madam, did you know you've left your gloves?

3 You are walking along the street. A man in front of you drops a £5 note. (*Pause*)
  sr Excuse me. Did you know you've dropped a £5 note?

4 You are walking along the street, and you see a man who has just parked in a no-parking area. (*Pause*)
  sr I say, I don't know if you knew, but this is a no-parking area.

5 You are in a restaurant. The lady at the next table is just leaving. Her umbrella is still hanging on the back of her chair. (*Pause*)
  sr Excuse me, madam. Did you know you've forgotten your umbrella?

6 You are in the library, where you aren't allowed to talk. A young couple are talking loudly. (*Pause*)
  sr I say, I hope you don't mind my saying so, but you aren't allowed to talk in here.

7 You are in a shop. A man is just leaving. His hat is on the counter. (*Pause*)
  sr Excuse me. Did you know you've forgotten your hat?

8 You are in the street. You can see a car with a puncture. Tell the driver. (*Pause*)
  sr Excuse me. I don't know if you knew, but you've got a puncture.

Notes on the tapescript

1 The comment is critical, so this pattern should be used to diminish aggressiveness.
2 You are doing her a service – neutral phrase.
3 As for 2.
4 This could be taken as being offensive – so a more elaborate form is needed.
5 As for 2.
6 Criticism is implied, so the elaborate form is needed.
7 As for 2.
8 This might be considered a bit nosey – he probably is aware of the puncture – so a more elaborate form is needed.

Exercise 4

This exercise should be self-explanatory. The questions are there to act as confirmations, like those given by Joanna in the model exchange. The ordering is temporal.

Tapescript

1 What sort of cake tins do I need? (*Pause*)
  sr Well, first of all you'll need two 20-cm sandwich tins, greased with butter and lined with greaseproof paper.
2 Right. What about the actual ingredients? (*Pause*)
  sr You need 175 grams of butter; 175 grams of caster sugar, warmed in the oven; 3 eggs at room temperature; and 175 grams of self-raising flour.
3 Good. Now, what do I do first? (*Pause*)
  sr First you mix the butter and the sugar in a bowl until the mixture's light and fluffy.
4 And what do I do then? (*Pause*)
  sr Then you beat the eggs one at a time and add them to the mixture. With the last egg you add a spoonful of flour.
5 What do I do after I've put the eggs in? (*Pause*)
  sr After you've put the eggs in, you sieve in the remaining flour and mix.
6 Now it's mixed, what do I do next? (*Pause*)
  sr Now it's mixed, you divide it equally between the tins.
7 And how long do I cook them, and at what temperature? (*Pause*)
  sr Cook them for 20–25 minutes in a pre-heated oven at 190°C.
8 How do I know when to take them out? (*Pause*)
  sr When you press lightly and the top feels springy, you take them out and leave them to cool on a rack.
9 Is that all? (*Pause*)
  sr No. When they are cool, sandwich them together with whipped cream and raspberry jam, and sprinkle the top with icing sugar.

Exercise 5

Ask students to suggest variants on the phrases reviewed. Allow them to add acceptable variants to their books, unless they appear in Unit 4 of Section B or Section C.

Pairwork, groupwork and roleplay suggestions

1 Use other recipes or students' favourite dishes. Give them recipes if they can't think of any. Recipes should be fairly simple; not too many ingredients or stages.
2 Try giving directions. Give students a map with a starting place. They take turns in asking for and giving directions to different places.
3 Give one student a map, and another student a blank sheet of squared paper. The first student gives directions to a particular place and the other student draws the map as he or she understands these directions. He or she indicates all the landmarks.

Unit 5 **Getting and giving opinions**

Checkpoint

Notes for guidance

1a This raises the question of an indirect approach to extracting opinions.

  b Joanna's question is deliberately imprecise in order to see how Henry is going to react. Henry's answer is not simply polite; it's an everyday way of giving a firm personal opinion.

Suggestion Students should continue this exchange as Henry or Joanna, but using far more direct language. *Do you want . . . ?*, *No, I don't*, etc. Compare the different outcomes.

2a Much worse. We know by his use of, *nowhere near as good.* Introduce and/or practise use of this phrase.

  b The use of *it seems* allows for late modification. Stress that Simon <u>is</u> sure of his belief; *it seems* does <u>not</u> weaken the force of his opinion.

3a Percy and Arnold are probably teachers.

  b The continuation will be based on Arnold's dissatisfaction.

  c *I don't want to be difficult* indicates that he is going to be difficult. (Ask for similar British 'hypocrisies', e.g., *I don't want to interrupt!*) *Leaves a lot to be desired* is a slightly formal or older person's way of saying that he dislikes something. Continuation is therefore likely to be bumbling, unless Percy shares the dissatisfaction.

Roleplay Ask students to continue this exchange, with Percy in favour of the new timetable, and then with Percy not in favour of it.

4 Because Simon doesn't want to give a direct and negative response. He wants to disguise his opinion without telling a lie.

Suggestion Make up a similar exercise using students' clothes and other items in the classroom. Students should respond to the opinions given.

5 It demonstrates the British way of apologising for a strong opinion. It begins with *sorry* and ends with *terrible.*

6a This is not an area where Sally expects a right or wrong answer, hence the use of the more emotional and less intellectual *feel*. Ask students for similar uses of *feel.*

  b David's long answer is possibly due to (1) having to think his way through his answer as he speaks – a form of hesitation, (2) his own character, (3) wanting to judge Sally's reaction to his opinion before completing it.

  c Point out that he changes course after the first sentence; hence the use of *personally* to limit opinion very much to himself alone, and then the use of *do* to give extra emphasis. Also point out David's form of apology: *I'm rather cautious, as you know!* Humour reduces the strength of David's speech; it's not to be taken too seriously.

7   *Well* . . . gives you time to think. Demonstrate the force of giving opinions without *Well* . . . They become far more aggressive. The use of *Well* . . . is to be encouraged.

8   The phrase not used is, *In my opinion*. It sounds stilted and rather pompous, and is not a normal way of introducing an opinion in current English. Emphasise the naturalness of *it seems to me* and its greater flexibility.

Students should listen to the model exchanges on the cassette, and then repeat and practise.

Exercise 1

Note   All the phrases can be strong. Do not let students think that indirect language equals indecisiveness or lack of an opinion. Also emphasise the need for this indirectness at all times, not just on polite occasions.
Supplementary exercise   Ask students to provide written continuations of the phrases, then practise saying them aloud. Monitor for intonation and communicative effectiveness.

Exercise 2

Suggested answers are as in the tapescript of Exercise 3. Practise introducing opinions with different beginnings. Monitor for difference in tone and effect.

Exercise 3

Remember to pause the cassette recorder to give students time to answer each question.

Tapescript
1   What do you think about that wonderful ad for X-ray cigarettes on TV?
    You think all cigarette advertising is a bad thing. (*Pause*)
    SR I'm sorry, but I think they're all unacceptable – good or bad!
2   What's your view on the British Council's book exhibitions?
    You think it's very difficult to get the English books you want in your country. (*Pause*)
    SR Well, if you ask me, it would be more useful if they did something about improving distribution.

3 Do you like this train set I got for Philip's third birthday?
You think parents generally spend too much on toys for their children. (*Pause*)
sr Don't you think it's a bit too much for that age?
4 Do you think that records will one day take over from live concerts altogether?
You think live music is much better than records or cassettes. (*Pause*)
sr Well, it seems to me that nothing could really do that completely.
5 How do you feel about contributing to old Fred's present?
You think the present your friends have bought for a colleague who is leaving is terrible! (*Pause*)
sr Well, I don't want to be difficult, but I do feel that it's not exactly what I would have chosen.
6 What's your view on living in a flat?
(*You think*) Living in a flat is much better than living in a house. (*Pause*)
sr Well, it seems to me there are many advantages to it.

Notes on the tapescript

1 sr should indicate strength of belief.
2 sr conveys frustration.
3 sr indicates criticism disguised by the question form. But the question form is genuine, so watch for the rise at the end of *age?*
4 Check the falling pattern of the whole sentence, and no pause between *it* and *completely*. Hesitation after *Well*.
5 Compare *Well* with its use in (4). Here it is said more positively, as a warning of the strength of opinion coming. Perhaps there is a slight trace of sarcasm in, *not exactly what I would have chosen*. Depends on how much stress you put on *I*.
6 Check that this open, direct question is in no way weakened or obscured by use of *it seems to me*. Use the sr on tape as a model for other opinions of this kind.

Exercise 4

Pause the tape after the beep to give students time to respond.

Tapescript

1 You want to know what your friend Sally thinks about the problem of unemployment in the world. You say:
sr What do you think about the problem of world umemployment, Sally?
2 You're interested in how your colleague Brian reacts to news of changes in your organisation's administration. You say:
sr What do you feel about the changes in administration, Brian?
3 You want to get your friend Richard's reaction to a new and very fashionable suit you've just bought. You say:
sr Do you like my new suit, Richard?
4 You're interested to hear what your teacher, Mr Clark, thinks about a new way of learning English called the Carrot method. You say:

sr Mr Clark, what's your view on the new Carrot method of learning English?

Now you must respond to the opinions requested.

5 What do you think about this scheme to rebuild the city centre? (*Pause*)
sr Well, if you ask me, it's a very good idea.

6 Do you think that young people are happier than their parents? (*Pause*)
sr Well, it seems to me that a lot of them are – but some aren't!

7 I've decided to ask everyone to take their summer holiday in October this year. Is that all right with you? (*Pause*)
sr Well, I don't want to be difficult, but I do feel that October is a bit late for a summer holiday.

8 How do you think the new government legislation will affect our business in the next few years? (*Pause*)
sr Well, as far as I can see, it won't affect us much.

9 Well, I think we should ask Aunt Jane to the wedding, but I know you feel very strongly that we shouldn't, isn't that so? (*Pause*)
sr Yes, I'm sorry, but I do feel that Aunt Jane is the last person I want to see at my wedding.

10 There's no doubt that it's a very complicated problem – but what do you think? Should we accept the offer, or should we suggest another alternative? (*Pause*)
sr Well, it seems to me that we should accept the offer.

Notes on the tapescript

Many alternatives are acceptable. Check and censure aggression in language forms and/or intonation patterns.
The srs were chosen for the following reasons:

1 This is a straightforward request to a friend, so it needs a direct question.

2 An emotional response is sought, hence the use of *feel*. *Think* would also be acceptable here.

3 This is again a request to a friend, so the question is direct. A possible alternative is, *What do you think of my new suit?*

4 Note the use of *Mr* in a more formal context, and the slightly more intellectual approach of *What's your view on . . . ?*

Questions 5–10 Concentrate on introductions to opinions and students' ability to give themselves time to think, using hesitation devices from Unit 1.

5 This is a public issue, hence the more formal *if you ask me* is used.

6 There is no right or wrong answer, so *it seems to me* is used to indicate flexibility on the part of the speaker.

7 The request is not popular, hence a stronger response is used. Point out the use of *a bit* to take the edge off negative opinion without reducing the impact.

8 sr suggests an incomplete grasp of the whole problem. Opinion is given on what <u>is</u> known. Ask students to think of other situations where this form would be useful.

9 Revise the use of apology before strong opinion. Ask for further examples.

10 Revise definite opinion preceded by, *It seems to me.*

Exercise 5

Ask students to suggest variants on the phrases given. Refer back, if necessary, to the note on *in my opinion.* Allow them to add acceptable variations in their books unless they appear in Unit 5 of Section B or Section C.

Pairwork suggestions   Be careful to restrict language practice as far as possible to getting and giving opinions – not agreeing or disagreeing. List of opinions to get:

 Friend's view of a new car
 Child's view of <u>his</u> new toy car
 Grandmother's view of youth of today
 Teenager's view of adults and/or parents

List of opinions to give:
 Your view on telephone privacy
 Your view on local drinking–driving laws
 Your view on ice-skating competitions
 Your view on the Olympic Games: political or apolitical?
 Your views on prices of hotels/restaurants in London/Tokyo, etc.

Unit 6 (Part 1) **Agreeing**

Checkpoint

Notes for guidance

1a (i) Wholeheartedly.
 b David's repeated, *Right . . . right* could be taken as showing a
   change in attitude, i.e. becoming more hesitant in his agreement,
   but in this exchange it is more likely to be a short definite
   agreement, designed to allow the other person to continue to give
   his opinion. David's first phrase is of course complete agreement.

2a Simon is not as positive as David, e.g. his use of *suppose* and the
   introductory *Well.*
 b He becomes slightly more positive in his second speech; perhaps
   he agrees reluctantly. Of the two intonation patterns, the first –
   fall+rise, fall on *suppose*, rise on *so* – indicates that Simon is not
   sure that Janet is right. There is a hesitancy in agreement; a lack of
   commitment. The second pattern – low-fall on *right* – indicates a
   reluctance to agree, but an acceptance that the other person is
   definitely right. This form is often used when you have changed
   your mind.
Pairwork   Ask students to continue this exchange.

3a Joanna becomes increasingly positive in her agreement.
 b Her *Mmm* indicates initial uncertainty; the intonation pattern is
   fall-rise. When students practise this in pairs, monitor for
   certainty or lack of it.
 d Joanna becomes increasingly interested as Frank proceeds; she
   warms to her task. Student readings should reflect this.
 e *Roleplay*   Ask students for their ideas on how this conversation
   might continue. Ask them to act out this continuation as Joanna
   and Frank, then as different characters, e.g. David and Brian, etc.

4   David is the most positive, then Joanna – by the end of the
   exchange. Simon is still unsure at the end of his exchange.

Play the model exchanges on the cassette for the students to listen to,
repeat and practise. Monitor for intonation, etc.

Exercise 1

Supplementary exercise   Get the students to provide written
continuations of each phrase and then practise saying them aloud.
Monitor for tone, appropriateness and effect.

Exercise 2

Suggested answers are as in the tapescript for Exercise 3 below. Any deviant responses should be examined for tone, appropriateness and effect.

Exercise 3

Remember to pause the cassette recorder to give students time to respond.

Tapescript

1 Of course, smoking is bad for your health. (*Pause*)
sr I couldn't agree more.
2 If all the world spoke English, there'd be fewer international misunderstandings. (*Pause*)
sr That's a good point.
3 I always say you don't succeed without hard work. (*Pause*)
sr Well, I suppose you're right.
4 Of course, one of the main problems in the world is unemployment . . . (*Pause*)
sr Right.
5 And because they're unemployed, people can't afford to buy goods . . . (*Pause*)
sr Mmm.
6 So the factories can't increase production . . . (*Pause*)
sr Quite.
7 And because they can't increase production, they can't take on more workers . . . (*Pause*)
sr Yes, of course.
8 All passengers should wear seat belts. (*Pause*)
sr Yes, you're absolutely right.
9 I often think the phone's more trouble than it's worth. (*Pause*)
sr Yes, I suppose so.

Notes on the tapescript

1 This is a generally agreed opinion, so the answer should show conviction.
2 sr implies general agreement without implying total and specific agreement. The intonation should show enthusiasm: fall+rise on *That's* and *point*.
3 This shows reluctant agreement. There could be a slight hesitation after *Well*. Intonation: fall+rise on <u>*suppose*</u> and *right*.
4–7 This is a continuous sequence.
4 Elicits short, non-interrupting assent.
5 This does the same.
6 Short and firm agreement.

7 Slightly more relaxed agreement.

Students should practise these four exchanges as one continuous exchange.

8 Nuclear stress. High-fall on _absolutely_, not on _right_.

9 The lengthening of _-pose_ in _suppose_ indicates uncertainty.

Exercise 4

Remember to pause the cassette recorder to give students time to respond.

Tapescript

Here are the first two opinions. Give short answers – you want the conversation to continue.

1 People spend too much money on cigarettes. (_Pause_)
  SR Right.
2 Pollution's a big problem in some cities. (_Pause_)
  SR Yes.

You're not completely sure if you agree with the next two opinions.

3 . . . and perhaps it would be better if back-seat passengers had to wear seat-belts too. (_Pause_)
  SR Well, I suppose so.
4 Well, there's no doubt that nowadays most people seem to prefer watching football on TV to going to the match. (_Pause_)
  SR Yes, I suppose you're right.

In the next two, you agree with what the speaker has said so far. You will have time to agree before he or she continues.

5 Television has totally changed our view of the world, hasn't it? (_Pause_)
  SR Yes, of course.
  And by the end of the century, video will have changed it even further.
6 Of course, the only problem with video is how expensive it is to buy. (_Pause_)
  SR That's a good point.
  But by the end of the century it will be as cheap as a transistor.

You agree totally with the last two opinions.

7 Parking's becoming impossible in most cities. (_Pause_)
  SR You're absolutely right.
8 Travelling certainly broadens your outlook. (_Pause_)
  SR I couldn't agree more.

Notes on the tapescript

1 and **2**   Any short agreeing phrases are acceptable. Check for level of enthusiasm; reject flat or bored intonation.

3 and **4**   Monitor for hesitancy in responses. See the intonation notes for Exercise 3.

5 and **6**   The answers are interchangeable. Don't stop the tape; the pause time is included, and overlong responses will thus be curtailed by the tape continuation.

7 and **8**   The answers are interchangeable. Check for firmness in agreement. See the intonation notes for Exercise 3.

Exercise 5

Ask students to suggest variants on the phrases reviewed. Allow them to add acceptable variants to their books, unless they appear in Unit 6 of Section B or Section C.

Unit 6 (Part 2) **Disagreeing**

Checkpoint

Notes for guidance

1a No, he doesn't.

  b This *yes* is a common and automatic British reaction implying understanding of the other person's meaning. See the notes on *Yes, but . . .*

  c Jim disagrees strongly with Frank's statement. His *Yes, but . . .* by no means weakens the force of this disagreement.

2a Richard also disagrees quite strongly. His *perhaps* shows only that he does not want to cause offence. His rejection of Shirley's opinion here takes the form of an extension to her argument.

  b Yes, his disagreement is expressed as forcibly as her opinion, his *perhaps* balancing her *If you ask me*. Both can be produced quite energetically.

  c No.

Roleplay Ask your students to continue the exchange in the characters of Richard and Shirley, and then as themselves. Richard is not keen to continue this line of conversation, so it should be reflected in the student roleplays.

3a The point here is that they could be business acquaintances or close friends (though not strangers, of course.).

  b Simon's *Well, you have a point there*, and *Yes, I see what you mean*, are part of normal social intercourse, not extreme politeness, and are said to introduce a disagreement without causing offence or ill-feeling. He certainly does not want to show agreement in this exchange. His 'reasonable' tone is not to be interpreted as weakness.

Roleplay Ask students to continue the exchange in the character of Simon or Brian.

4a Justin disagrees strongly with Beatrice, who gives her opinions in a very direct and forthright manner. But his disagreements, whilst firm, avoid being rude. Note that he apologises before voicing his complete disagreement. See also the notes on disagreeing at the beginning of this unit in the Student's Book.

  b If the conversation were to continue, Beatrice would have to become even more positive, and Justin more direct in his disagreement. It is more likely that the conversation would move to a different and hopefully less controversial topic.

Roleplay Ask students to continue the conversation as Beatrice and Justin. Monitor closely the progress of the continuation, and the degree of 'heatedness' that both parties achieve. NB. This to be done only after the whole unit has been studied.

Play the model exchanges on the cassette for the students to listen to, repeat and practise. Monitor for intonation, etc.

Exercise 1

Supplementary exercise   Get students to produce written continuations of each phrase and then practise saying each one aloud. Monitor for tone, appropriateness and effect.

Exercise 2

Suggested answers are as in the tapescript for Exercise 3 below. Any deviant responses should be examined for differences in tone, appropriateness and effect.

Exercise 3

Remember to pause the cassette recorder to give students time to respond.

Tapescript

1 I think city centres should be traffic-free zones. (*Pause*)
   sr I see what you mean, but it would be difficult to move around.
2 We should all take more exercise, in my view. (*Pause*)
   sr That's quite true, but it's so difficult to find time.
3 Pop music is destroying people's interest in classical music. (*Pause*)
   sr Perhaps, but don't you think that classical music is less interesting anyway?
4 I think boxing is terrible! It's so dangerous! (*Pause*)
   sr Yes, but don't you think that people should be allowed to box if they want to?
5 Everyone should speak English all over the world. The other languages are a waste of time! (*Pause*)
   sr I'm sorry, I just can't agree with you.
6 Cigarettes should be banned completely. (*Pause*)
   sr Well, you have a point, but that would be pretty hard to do!
7 Speed limits are crazy. People should drive at whatever speed they like. (*Pause*)
   sr I really can't agree with you on that!
8 Everyone in England is too fat! They should all go on a diet! (*Pause*)
   sr Oh surely not! Some English people are quite thin!

Notes on the tapescript

Continuations to the disagreement phrases have been provided as an aid to intonation and a guide to appropriateness. Many disagreement phrases are possible in each case. Monitor for calm and non-aggressive intonation in each case.

1 Check for fall-rise on *mean* followed by a slight pause before the continuation.
2 Check equal accents on *That's* and *quite*, and nuclear fall-rise on *true*. The second clause has high pre-head, high head on *difficult*, high-fall nucleus on *time*.
3 and 4 The examples have been chosen to elicit qualified disagreement. Over-reaction would be inappropriate here.
5 This is clearly an extreme opinion, directly put. SR gives strong but calm disagreement. Here, a more discreet form of disagreement would be inappropriate.
6 This statement has a basis in sense – cigarettes are unhealthy – but it is an extreme and impractical suggestion. SR admits strength of feeling and possible justification for it, whilst introducing a disagreement with its specific aims.
7 and 8 These disagreeing phrases are interchangeable; both are reactions to extreme and ill-conceived opinions. Monitor for firmness of tone without harshness or aggression.

Exercise 4

Remember to pause the cassette recorder to give students time to respond.

Tapescript

1 Everything on television is a complete load of rubbish! (*Pause*)
SR Oh, surely not!
2 Sport must be one of the most stupid activities anyone can get involved in! (*Pause*)
SR I really can't agree with you on that!
3 The weather in England is fabulous, isn't it? (*Pause*)
SR I don't think I can agree with you on that!
4 Nobody's really unemployed unless they want to be – they all enjoy lazing around at home, that's all. (*Pause*)
SR I'm sorry, I just can't agree with you.
5 Rich people only get rich by luck. Hard work doesn't come into it. (*Pause*)
SR Yes, but a lot of rich people work very hard, don't they?
6 Women's liberation is a really stupid idea. It's obvious that women aren't the same as men. (*Pause*)
SR I see what you mean, but women should have equal rights, don't you think?
7 Animals are filthy creatures – and people shouldn't have them in the house as pets. All they do is spread disease. (*Pause*)
SR Well, you have a point, but animals can be very good companions, particularly to old people.
8 Single-sex schooling is the only sensible form of education – mixing boys with girls is asking for trouble! (*Pause*)

SR: Perhaps, but don't you think that keeping the sexes apart is also asking for trouble?

Notes on the tapescript

Many alternatives are possible. The SRs were chosen for the following reasons:

1 This is an extreme, short opinion eliciting a short, firm, but polite rejection.
2 This is another extreme opinion, but slightly more formally expressed, and provokes a slightly longer, but just as firm a disagreement phrase.
3 This mistaken opinion receives a slightly laconic response; good-humoured disagreement is essential here.
4 This is another extreme opinion. Note the apology before the speaker admits his/her inability to agree.
5 *Yes, but . . .* is here used to introduce an immediate and contradictory point of view, directly counter-balancing the original opinion.
6 This statement is half true: women are not the *same* as men. SR admits this but then allows for contrary opinion, ending with a request for agreement. The student's response should provide similar balanced disagreement, and also the possibility of continuing the dialogue as in the SR.
7 Again, the statement contains a partial truth. SR admits this whilst disagreeing by pointing out the advantages of pets.
8 As for (6) and (7).

Exercise 5

Ask students to suggest variants on the phrases reviewed. They should enter them in their books, unless they appear in Unit 6 of Section B or Section C.

Pairwork, groupwork and roleplay suggestions

Refer back to the students' written continuations of the phrases in Exercise 1 (supplementary exercise). In the light of subsequent practice (Exercises 2, 3, 4, and 5), ask them to use these monitored sentences as the basis for conversation in groups or pairs, extending or developing their original ideas.

Unit 7 **Getting what you want, making requests, giving and refusing permission**

Checkpoint

Notes for guidance

1a It is very difficult to ascribe status from this short exchange. It assumes a degree of equality with politeness, which is the norm for any British exchange of this nature.

b *Yes, sure* would perhaps be less used by elderly people. The point of this exchange, though, is to demonstrate that this is absolutely standard British English.

2a Again, this is a very standard British exchange. The two speakers obviously know each other, but not intimately.

b Hence the use of *could*, where *can* would be used with intimate friends and *may* in more formal, hierarchical situations.

c The intonation pattern is low pre-head, fall-rise nucleus. A completely falling pattern would indicate bad temper.

3a Because his request is for something his father may not wish to agree to; in other words, he uses more indirect language when approaching a more difficult task.

b His father is not an authoritarian figure, (see above on *sure*), but even so the son needs to approach him carefully with this request.

4a Not very well.

b But Bruce clearly does genuinely want to see George's model soldier collection; he uses requesting forms at the beginning and the end of his utterance to make that plain.

c We know as soon as George says *Actually* that there is a problem, and thus he is probably going to refuse the request.
Note   *Actually* as a warning word is dealt with in several units.

d George's second sentence is an explanation for refusing the request. Stress that in 90 per cent of refusals in English it is imperative to give a reason for the refusal.

Roleplay   Students should continue this dialogue as Bruce and George.

5   and **6a** The slight formality of *could* plus the tag *do you think?* indicates that the speakers in (5) do not know each other very well. In (6) the speakers are equals, perhaps at work or college, but not necessarily friends.

b (5) and (6) could both have taken place at a workplace or school/college.

c (5) comes in mid-conversation (situation), (6) at the beginning of a conversation.

7 and **8** The request in (8) is obviously more important than that in (7).

  a (7) shows a subordinate asking permission of an employer, hence the use of *May*.

  b Both these exchanges took place at a workplace.

  c (7) comes at the beginning of a conversation, (8) in mid-conversation (the tentative *Do you think . . . ?* would probably be preceded by lead-in utterances).

  d Mr Seagrove's direct, *Yes, all right* suggests he is not happy with Beverley leaving early. If he were, he would have said *Yes, of course. Go ahead.* or *Certainly.*

Play the model exchanges on the cassette for the students to listen to, repeat and practise. Monitor for intonation, etc.

Exercise 1

Supplementary exercise Get students to provide written continuations of each phrase and then practise saying them aloud. Monitor for tone, appropriateness and effect.

Exercise 2

Suggested request forms for A–H:
A–1 *Excuse me, have you got any change for the telephone?*
B–4 *Do you think I could have some more coffee/another cake?*
C–8 *Sorry to bother you, but have you got the time?*
D–2 *Could I borrow your dictionary?*
E–3 *Would you open the door for me, please?*
F–7 *I'd very much like to see your stamp collection.*
G–6 *Do you think you could give me a lift to the station?*
H–5 *Could I borrow your umbrella, do you think?*
Any deviant responses should be examined for differences in effect and appropriateness.
Note This exercise is not used as the basis for Exercise 3 that follows. As requests and acceptances/refusals are normally short activities, more directed practice has been given in place of roleplay suggestions.

Exercise 3

Tapescript

1 Ask a colleague if you can borrow his pen. (*Pause*)
  sr Could I borrow your pen?
2 Ask a new friend if you can see his record collection. You know it's a very good one. (*Pause*)

sʀ I'd very much like to see your record collection.
3 Ask your secretary to type two copies of a letter for you. Her name is Sally.
  (*Pause*)
  sʀ Would you type two copies of this letter, Sally?
4 Now ask Sally if she could type a hundred copies of a letter! (*Pause*)
  sʀ Sally, do you think you could type a hundred copies of this letter?
5 Knock on your flatmate's door and ask if you can borrow some coffee. She's
  trying to write some letters. (*Pause*)
  sʀ Sorry to bother you, but could I borrow some of your coffee?
6 Stop someone in the street and ask him or her for the time. (*Pause*)
  sʀ Excuse me, have you got the time?
7 Ask your hostess if you can have another chicken sandwich – they're
  delicious! (*Pause*)
  sʀ Do you think I could have another chicken sandwich? They're delicious!
8 Ask your boss if you can have an hour off work this afternoon. You want to
  visit a friend in hospital. (*Pause*)
  sʀ Could I have an hour off work this afternoon, do you think? I want to
  visit someone in hospital.

Notes on the tapescript

In this unit the notes depend very much on the request forms chosen
by the students. Intonation patterns should be checked against sʀs
and/or those given in the model exchanges and model phrases. But, in
particular, check the difference in tone required for (3), a
straightforward request/command for an ordinary task, and (4), a more
persuasive or entreating tone required for a harder task. Check the use
of *Excuse me* to start any conversation with a stranger in (6). Check the
reason given for wanting an hour off work in the student's response in
(8).

Exercise 4

Tapescript

1 Can I borrow your pencil? (*Pause*)
  sʀ Sure.
2 Excuse me, could I use your telephone to make a long-distance call? (*Pause*)
  sʀ Erm, well . . . yes, all right. Go ahead.
3 I'd very much like to see that excellent essay you wrote. (*Pause*)
  sʀ Oh, by all means. I'll just go and get it.
4 Sorry to bother you, but is it all right to use the toilet now? (*Pause*)
  sʀ Yes, certainly. Go ahead.
Now refuse the next four requests. You will be given a reason for your refusal.
5 Do you think I could use your typewriter this afternoon?
  (*Whisper*) You need it yourself. (*Pause*)
  sʀ I'm sorry, I need it myself this afternoon.
6 Can I use the new video machine tomorrow?
  (*Whisper*) It's already booked by someone else. (*Pause*)
  sʀ I'm sorry, I'm afraid you can't. It's already booked.

7 Would you help me look for those missing books this afternoon?
   (*Whisper*) You've got to go to a meeting in town. (*Pause*)
   sr I can't, really – I've got to go to a meeting in town this afternoon.
8 Can I play my new record on your hi-fi?
   (*Whisper*) It's not working properly.
   sr Actually, you can't, because it's not working properly at the moment.

Notes on the tapescript

Many variants are possible. The srs were chosen for the following reasons:
1 The simple request requires a simple and short acceptance.
2 The hesitation is due to the possible expense to be incurred. Immediate acceptance would be unlikely.
3 This flattering request brings a wholehearted acceptance.
4 sr implies sympathy with first speaker's problem – the tone should reflect this.
5 sr does not actually contain a direct refusal. An explanation is inserted instead. This is a very common short form of refusal.
6 Note the use of *I'm sorry* with *I'm afraid* for added emphasis in certain difficult situations.
7 sr shows regret at not accepting – *I can't, really* followed by immediate explanation. Note the high-head plus low-rise nucleus on *I can't, really*. Compare the difference in effect of *I really can't*, which indicates complete refusal.
8 *Actually* could also be the third word in this sentence. sr has it as the first word where it serves as a warning.

Exercise 5

Ask students to suggest variants on the phrases reviewed. Allow them to add acceptable variants to their books, unless they appear in Unit 7 of Section B or Section C.

Pairwork, groupwork and roleplay suggestions

Request the following from colleagues, friends, children, etc: stamps, change, bicycles, headphones, books, records, video machines etc., and any classroom object. Students should accept and refuse requests in pairs, remembering to explain refusals.

Unit 8 Inviting, suggesting, accepting and refusing

Checkpoint

Notes for guidance

1a Janet and Richard are friends or possibly colleagues.

b Richard uses first names, but the slightly formal *I was wondering . . . ?*

c Janet is accepting. Her two responses are the somewhat formal way of accepting, appropriate to *I was wondering . . . ?*

Roleplay The dialogue can be continued . . . *We'd love to come.* Then establish the time, how to get there, etc. (See Unit A4 for directions.)

2 Linda and David are probably colleagues. Linda uses a polite indirect way when asking David for a suggestion.

3a Justin and Joanna know each other quite well; his invitation is direct.

b No, she doesn't.

c This is a standard way of refusing so as not to give offence.

d No, she doesn't. *Thanks all the same* is used in refusals only.

4 David.

Play the model exchanges on the cassette for the students to listen to, repeat and practise. Monitor for intonation, etc.

Exercise 1

The phrases examined in this unit are generally uttered in the upper part of the voice range. The suggestion forms all have a high-fall pattern.

Supplementary exercise Get students to provide written continuations of each phrase and then practise saying them aloud. Monitor for tone, appropriateness and effect.

Exercise 2

Suggested answers are as in the tapescript for Exercise 3 below. Any deviant responses should be examined for differences in tone, appropriateness and effect.

Exercise 3

Remember to pause the cassette recorder to give students time to respond. Remember the intonation note to Exercise 1.

Tapescript

1 Would you like to come for a drink? (*Pause*)
  SR I'd love to, but I'm afraid I can't.
2 I was wondering if you'd like to come out with me one day? (*Pause*)
  SR That's very kind of you.
3 Why don't we go to an Indian restaurant and have dinner? (*Pause*)
  SR That would be lovely.
4 Perhaps we could have lunch in a pub. (*Pause*)
  SR I'm afraid I can't. Thanks all the same.
5 Would you like something more to eat? (*Pause*)
  SR Thank you very much.
6 I've got two tickets for the Cliff Richard concert on Saturday. Would you like to come? (*Pause*)
  SR That's very kind of you, but I'm afraid I'm busy. Thanks all the same.
7 Would you like to come and spend the weekend with us in the country? (*Pause*)
  SR I'd like that very much.
8 What about coming round to dinner with us after the film this evening? (*Pause*)
  SR We'd love to.

Notes on the tapescript

Remember the intonation note to Exercise 1.
1 The invitation is a basic form, so the response should be basic. In fact the almost automatic response to *Would you like . . . ?* is *I'd love to*. We have chosen to refuse and have used the equivalent form.
2 The invitation is elaborate and requires a similar response. *I'd like that very much* would be a possible acceptance, but it is perhaps too eager in tone compared to the invitation.
3 The use of this suggestion form means that either the subject of dinner is under discussion (it is the Indian restaurant which is put forward as the suggestion, which means that none of the refusal forms given is suitable), or that it is dinner-time. In the latter case, however, as it is a suggestion and not an invitation, *Thanks all the same* is not a suitable response. From a syntactic point of view, *I'd love to* is not a suitable response to this suggestion form, so we can't use *I'd love to, but I'm afraid I can't*. These points also eliminate most of the acceptances. *I'd like that very much* is too elaborate, which leaves us with *That would be lovely*. We have chosen the acceptance.
4 Again, this is a suggestion rather than an invitation. *I'd love to, but I'm afraid I can't* would be an alternative refusal, but see note 1. For an acceptance, *That would be lovely* would be the most suitable, but see note 3.
5 Since *Would you like* is followed by *something*, the answer cannot be *I'd love to*. *That's very kind of you* is too elaborate for this invitation, hence *Thank you very much*.

6 See note 3. Here we have a specific date given, so the negative response is possible. For a positive response, use *That would be lovely*. To use it here would give problems with the rest of the exercise, however.

7 This is a substantial invitation, so the elaborate response is the most suitable. For a refusal, a development along the lines of *That's very kind of you, but I'm . . .* would be necessary.

8 The suggestion implies that you are all going to the cinema together. This makes the refusal forms inappropriate. *That would be lovely* would be an alternative, but see note 3.

Exercise 4

Tapescript

1 There is a new member of staff, Marian, in your office. You would like to get to know her. Invite her to lunch with you. (*Pause*)
  sr I was wondering if you would like to come to lunch with me, Marian?

2 One of your colleagues has been invited to dinner by the manager and his wife. He wants to take a gift, but doesn't know what. Make a suggestion. (*Pause*)
  sr Why don't you take his wife a box of chocolates?

3 Your friend doesn't like your idea. Suggest something else. (*Pause*)
  sr Perhaps you could take a bunch of flowers.

4 You enjoyed your lunch with Marian. Perhaps you could spend an evening together sometime over the weekend? (*Pause*)
  sr Would you like to come out to dinner on Saturday?

5 Are you doing anything this Sunday? Would you like to go to Brighton for the day?
  Accept. (*Pause*)
  sr That's very kind of you. I'd love to.

6 I'm going to the Museum of London on Saturday afternoon. What about coming with me?
  Refuse. (*Pause*)
  sr I'd love to, but I'm afraid I'm busy. Thanks all the same.

7 I was wondering if you'd like to come to the cinema with me this evening. There's a new James Bond film on at the Odeon.
  Accept eagerly. (*Pause*)
  sr I'd like that very much.

8 Perhaps we could have a bite to eat after the film.
  Accept. (*Pause*)
  sr That would be lovely.

Notes on the tapescript

Remember the use of the upper part of the vocal range. See the intonation note to Exercise 1.

1 You don't know her. Use the elaborate form.

2 This is the first suggestion form to use.

3 Second or alternative suggestion form.
4 You have been out together, so a more basic form can be used.
5 This is a basic invitation, so it needs a basic response.
6 This is a straightforward refusal.
7 Eager acceptance is expressed. See note 2, Exercise 3.
8 The suggestion is accepted.

Pairwork, groupwork and roleplay suggestions

Students in groups try to decide what to do one evening or weekend. Each puts forward different suggestions and they are refused or modified until the group as a whole accepts.

Unit 9 **Approving and disapproving**

Checkpoint

Notes for guidance

1a No. Arthur's greeting, *Good evening*, is too formal for husband to wife.

b The word order has been chosen for emphasis – on *dress*, not the wearing of it.

c Daphne has not necessarily had the dress for years; she is demonstrating a common, slightly embarrassed reaction to a compliment or flattery.

d Intonation of Arthur's next statements is: low pre-head with high head on *Really* and high-fall nucleus on *fabulous*. In the second sentence, high-head on *Red*, high-fall nucleus on *really*, low tail.

2a No. *Fantastic* is here used to mean very good, exciting – not unbelievable, unusual or indeed anything to do with 'fantasy'.

b Peter was not impressed by the film – note his *I suppose* and colloquial *I wouldn't rush!* (*to see it, if I were you, because it isn't that good.*)

Roleplay   Ask the students to continue this exchange.

3a Of course not. The question draws attention to the colloquial phrase *How is it going?* used in a variety of situations to ask for someone's opinion or reaction to a new acquisition or activity, e.g. *How is the new lawn-mower going?* or *How are your English studies going?*

b Henry is happier than he expected to be. His *Well, d'you know* at the beginning of his reply indicates his own surprise at the success of the swimming pool.

Roleplay   Ask the students to continue this dialogue as the characters shown, and then as themselves.

4a Janet and Simon do know each other well: they could even be husband and wife. Less intimate friends would be more circumspect in giving opinions on the other's dress, particularly man to woman.

b Even so, Simon feels obliged to say that he is *not sure* he likes Janet's green shoes as a euphemism for *I don't like the green shoes*, or, *The green shoes don't go with the rest of the outfit*.

c He does not apologise for giving her good advice; he apologises for having to cause her difficulties whilst not changing or weakening his disapproval – a useful ploy.

Roleplay   Ask the students to create similar dialogues as husbands and wives, girlfriends and boyfriends, etc. Monitor for intonation and appropriateness of language produced.

5a The phrases are: *really amazing; I really like that; quite good; I can't say I like . . .; I really don't like . . .; I can't stand . . .; I think it's absolutely awful.*

  b Roger's reply is sarcastic, and he is rather taken aback. He probably wasn't expecting such a detailed appraisal.

  c They could be discussing a work of art, a painting or mobile perhaps. Use this for a discussion point and extension – how students would show approval or disapproval of different works of art, poetry, music, literature.

6a In a restaurant – not someone's house.

  b Quentin would like to think that he knows more about food than Amanda. See his first speech, which assumes a knowledge of the 'correct' taste of a sauce.

  c *Really, actually* and *absolutely* are used here as described in the introduction to this unit. Student answers to this question should be monitored to check understanding and assimilation of points made.

Roleplay   Students pretend to eat a restaurant meal and comment on good and bad dishes.

7 Arnold's intention is not to discourage Sally, hence the use of *Well, actually, rather, I'm afraid* and encouraging phrases, *never mind* and *it will do.*

8a Rick and Dave are adults, not children, and Dave is probably slightly older than Rick. His disapproval phrases, *I think . . .* and *I'm sorry, but . . .* are somewhat more circumspect than Rick's approval phrases, although both speakers would consider themselves to be talking plain, direct English.

  b They know each other well enough to speak to each other plainly, and could be older and younger brothers or close friends.

Roleplay   Students should continue the dialogue as Rick and Dave, then as themselves.

Play the model exchanges on the cassette for the students to listen to, repeat and practise. Monitor for intonation, etc.

Exercise 1

Supplementary exercise   Get students to provide written continuations of each phrase and then practise saying them aloud. Monitor for tone, appropriateness and effect.

Exercise 2

Suggested answers are as in the tapescript for Exercise 3. Any deviant responses should be examined for differences in tone, appropriateness and effect.

Exercise 3

Remember to pause the cassette recorder to give students time to respond.

Tapescript

1 Another cup of tea? And what do you think of that marzipan cake? (*Pause*)
   SR Er, actually, I don't really like it, I'm afraid.
2 What do you think about this new road plan, then, eh? (*Pause*)
   SR It's absolutely awful! It's going to take me twice as long to get to work if it goes through, you know.
3 Oh, I must ask you, what do you think of Sally's new car? She says it's terrific. (*Pause*)
   SR It's all right, I suppose. It seems about the same as her old one.
4 There you are, then. All done. Lovely shade of pink, that. (*Pause*)
   SR Er . . . look . . . I'm sorry, but I'm not sure I like it after all.
5 (On the phone.) Hello, is that you? Oh good. Listen, I've just been given two tickets for the opera next week. Do you want to come with me? (*Pause*)
   SR I'm sorry, but I can't stand that sort of thing.
6 What do you think about Doug and Rita getting married, then? (*Pause*)
   SR It's great, isn't it? I think they'll make each other really happy. After all, . . .
7 How's your home computer working out – is it as difficult to work with as you'd thought? (*Pause*)
   SR It's quite *good*, really! It's much easier to use than I thought, and it's terribly useful in all sorts of . . .
8 Tell me, is the local football team any good where you come from? (*Pause*)
   SR It's really fantastic! I mean, it's one of the best in the country, *I* think.

Notes on the tapescript

Monitor students' intonation against the SRs on the cassette. Note in particular:
1 Apologetic tone.
2 Strength of disapproval.
3 Lack of enthusiasm in giving approval.
4 Fall-rise nucleus on *sorry*. Second phrase: low pre-head, high-head on *not*, with strong accents on *sure* and *like*, and a high-fall nucleus on *all*.
5 Replying to a friend allows frankness of disapproval; there is little or no hesitation between *sorry* and *but*. High-fall nucleus on *stand*.
6 Ensure enthusiastic tone in students' responses. Ask for continuation of approval at the end of the exercise.

7 sr assumes surprised approval. Check nucleus: fall+rise on *good* and
really.

8 sr assumes still more enthusiasm on *really*. There are two tone
groups: *It's really* with high-fall pattern, and *fantastic*, also with high-
fall intonation pattern. This is in order to convince the questioner,
so a degree of over-acting should be encouraged here.

Exercise 4

Remind students to speak when they hear the beep. Pause the cassette
recorder to give them time to respond to the situation described before
listening to the suggested response.

Tapescript

1 Your friend Ralph arrives in a brand new white suit. He clearly thinks it's
very good. (*Beep*)
sr That's a fantastic suit, Ralph! Where did you get it?

2 A colleague at work has just bought a new calculator. It's better than yours,
but you don't want to seem jealous when you tell him you like it. (*Beep*)
sr I quite like your new calculator.

3 Your sister is going out with Louis tonight. You think his jokes are very bad,
so when your sister asks why you don't like him, you reply . . . (*Beep*)
sr I can't stand his dreadful jokes!

4 Your fellow students are arranging a surprise party for Neville. You know
he's very shy and hates parties. They ask what you think of the plan. You
say . . . (*Beep*)
sr I don't think it's a very good idea, actually. Neville's very shy and . . .

5 You've just finished an excellent meal. What do you say to your hostess,
Pauline? (*Beep*)
sr Pauline, that was really delicious! A really fabulous meal!

6 And what would Pauline, your hostess, say if in fact it was her husband
Dennis who had cooked the meal? (*Beep*)
sr Er, well, *actually* it was Dennis who cooked it, not me!

7 You've just been reading the newspaper; there have been more terrorist
bombings. Your colleague asks, *What do you think about it?* You say . . .
(*Beep*)
sr It's absolutely appalling.

8 You had not been looking forward to moving to a smaller flat. But now you
have settled in, you find you rather like it after all. (*Beep*)
sr Well, it's not bad at all, really. It's close to town and the shops are really
good . . .

9 Friends visiting town want to know the name of a good restaurant. You
want to recommend Mario's, your favourite. You say . . . (*Beep*)
sr You *must* go to Mario's. It's really great. The food's terrific and the
service is absolutely excellent.

10 The same friends have heard Luigi's Restaurant is very good. The last time
you went there you walked out because the food was so bad. You say . . .
(*Beep*)

sr Oh no! It's absolutely dreadful! The food is quite disgusting and the service is absolutely appalling! You *can't* go there!

Notes on the tapescript

The situations call for varying degrees of approval and disapproval. The srs were chosen for the following reasons:

1 *Fantastic* here implies an excited and surprised reaction to the white suit.
2 Use of *quite like* shows reserved approval, but note the even accents on *quite* and *like*. A heavier accent on *like* would indicate firmer, but surprised approval.
3 You are on intimate terms with your sister, hence the directness of your disapproval. Acceptable alternatives would be, *His jokes are absolutely appalling*, or *He tells really terrible jokes*.
4 This revises *actually* as a warning <u>and</u> correcting word. Beginning with *I don't think* softens the blow of disapproval. Note that the second sentence offers a reason for disapproval.
5 sr demonstrates the hearty enthusiasm needed when showing approval in this situation. Practise intonation against the cassette when the whole exercise has been completed.
6 sr allows for hesitation and embarrassment, with *actually* drawn out in uncomfortable correction.
7 The situation is one which most of us find terrible. Even amongst strangers or superiors, a strong expression of disapproval would be totally acceptable. Hence the sr we have given.
8 sr again shows surprised approval. The continuation gives reasons for approval where none was expected.
9 sr demonstrates the degree of over-acting needed when approving or recommending. Note the high-fall nucleus on *must*.
10 In contrast, the sr shows parallel over-acting when demonstrating disapproval. Replay these last two exchanges on the cassette for students to repeat, practise and do related pair work.

Exercise 5

Ask students to suggest variants on phrases reviewed. Allow them to add acceptable variants to their books, unless they appear in Section B or Section C of Unit 9.

Unit 10 **Apologising**

Checkpoint

Notes for guidance

1a It takes place in a restaurant or a pub.
  b Linda and Janet have never actually met before. Linda checks Janet's identity, using her surname.
  c Linda must be more than a few minutes late – enough to have to apologise and explain, and for Janet and Simon to have started without her.
  d No, she isn't.
  e Linda must accept Janet's apology for starting, with *I'm glad you did*, and then she will greet Simon.

2a Yes, David has lost the book.
  b No, it hasn't been handed in.
  c We use *seem* to soften the blow when apologising for something we have done. See the notes to the model phrases.
  d Yes, Joanna is upset.
  e Again, *I'm afraid* is used to soften the blow – here because she is telling him that he must find it or replace it immediately.

3a Brian and Richard are probably outside Brian's house. Richard is perhaps visiting one of Brian's neighbours.
  b Richard has parked his car too close to Brian's, and this is rather thoughtless and anti-social!
  c As Richard has been polite and apologetic, it would be offensive (to the British) for Brian not to respond in a similar manner.

Play the model exchanges on the cassette for the students to listen to, repeat and practise. Monitor for intonation, etc.

Exercise 1

Intonation notes

I'm sorry to be . . . etc. Fall+rise. Fall on *sorry*, rise on final stressed syllable.
I'm really sorry . . . etc. Fall+rise. Fall on emphasising word *really*. The alternative form found in the second exchange, *I really am sorry*, has the fall on *am* with emphatic stress.
I do apologise. Fall +rise. The *do* carries emphatic stress, and the fall is on *do*.
I hope you don't mind . . . Fall-rise. Upper part of voice range.
Supplementary exercise   Get students to provide written continuations

of each phrase and then practise saying them aloud. Monitor for tone, appropriateness and effect.

Exercise 2

Suggested answers are as in the tapescript for Exercise 3. Any deviant responses should be examined for differences in tone, appropriateness and effect.

Exercise 3

Remember to pause the cassette recorder to give students time to respond.

Tapescript

1 Oh hello . . . I, er . . . I wasn't expecting you so . . . er . . . (*Pause*)
  SR I hope you don't mind my dropping in like this.
2 Ah, here you are! I'm so glad you've made it. We were beginning to wonder if something had happened to you. (*Pause*)
  SR I'm sorry to be so late. I'm afraid my car wouldn't start.
3 Oh good! Nice to see you. I hope you've brought the book with you. (*Pause*)
  SR I'm really sorry. I seem to have left it at home.
4 Look out! . . . That's my drink . . . Oh drat! (*Pause*)
  SR I'm terribly sorry. That was clumsy of me. I hope it hasn't gone all over you.
5 What time did we say we would meet for the film? (*Pause*)
  SR I'm sorry. I'm afraid I won't be able to come on Saturday.
6 Ow! Look out! Do watch where you're going! (*Pause*)
  SR I do apologise. I hope you aren't hurt.
7 (sleepily) Hello, 234 5678. Who is it? (*Pause*)
  SR I hope you don't mind my ringing as late as this.
8 Simon Rogers? I'm afraid there's no one here of that name. (*Pause*)
  SR I do apologise. I seem to have got the wrong number.

Notes on the tapescript

See the intonation notes on the individual phrases.
1 This form is recommended in the model phrases. Since the second part is *my dropping . . .*, it must have *I hope you don't mind* as the first part, for syntactic reasons.
2 This is a basic apology. The second part is suitable only to this situation.
3 The choice between *I'm really sorry* and *I'm terribly sorry* is arbitrary here. See below.
4 Although the choice between *I'm really sorry* and *I'm terribly sorry* seems arbitrary, in the case of an accident like this, *terribly* sounds more natural. The rest of the apology is built into the situation.
5 Working back, only *be able to come . . .* fits this situation. It requires

I won't . . . hence *I'm afraid I won't.* The suitable phrase to precede this is merely, *I'm sorry.*

6 You need to apologise emphatically in such a situation.

7 The second part of the apology, built into the situation, presupposes the first.

8 An assertive apology is needed when you disturb someone in his or her own home.

Exercise 4

Tapescript

1 You have invited Janet Davidson round for a cup of coffee, but you've just discovered you've run out of coffee. Apologise and offer her some tea instead. (*Pause*)
   sᴿ I'm terribly sorry. I'm afraid I seem to have run out of coffee. Would you like a cup of tea instead?

2 Michael Conway has asked if he can come round and see you on Saturday evening. Unfortunately you will be out. Apologise and tell him. (*Pause*)
   sᴿ I'm sorry, but I'm afraid I'll be out then.

3 You promised faithfully you would try and finish some work for David by today. He is on the phone to find out if it's ready. Unfortunately you haven't done it. (*Pause*)
   sᴿ I do apologise. I'm afraid I haven't been able to do it.

4 You have been invited to a party. Justin has just come to stay with you, so you take him to the party too. Apologise for doing so without phoning first. (*Pause*)
   sᴿ I hope you don't mind my bringing Justin with me.

Now accept these apologies as you think fit.

5 I'm sorry to have kept you waiting so long. (*Pause*)
   sᴿ That's perfectly all right.

6 I hope you don't mind my coming round like this . . . (*Pause*)
   sᴿ Not at all.

7 I do apologise. I had no idea this seat was already taken. (*Pause*)
   sᴿ That's perfectly all right.

8 I'm terribly sorry, but I'm afraid I won't be able to come and do it for you after all. (*Pause*)
   sᴿ Oh well, I suppose that'll be all right.

Notes on the tapescript

1 This is rather an embarrassing situation, so a slightly stronger apology is needed.

2 There is no difficulty with this situation, so a basic apology will do.

3 It was a promise, so an assertive form is necessary.

4 It is normal to check if you can bring house-guests with you. See the note to the model phrases on *I hope you don't mind my -ing . . .*

5-7 These need straightforward acceptances. The choice of which form is arbitrary.

8 This requires a more grudging acceptance.

Exercise 5

Ask students to suggest variants on the phrases reviewed. Allow them to add acceptable variants to their books, unless they appear in Unit 10 of Section B or Section C.

Pairwork, groupwork and roleplay suggestions

1 Apologies can best be grouped with complaints (see Unit C9) for pairwork.

2 Students can practise apologies in more situations like the ones above.

3 Refer back to the students' written continuations of the phrases in Exercise 1 (supplementary exercise). In the light of subsequent practice (Exercises 2, 3, 4, 5), ask them to use these monitored sentences as the basis for conversation in pairs or groups, extending or developing their original ideas.

Section B
**English for formal
and public situations**

Unit 1 **Giving yourself time**

In this unit there is no diagram for linking items visually, and once more the choice of hesitation phrases in the exercises is arbitrary. But it is essential that students should use as many of them as possible, even though in this unit it may seem more artificial than in the same unit of Section A.

Checkpoint

Notes for guidance

1a Frank primarily needs to work out his answer to a rather difficult question, though knowing the direction of Janet's thoughts may help him. So the answer is mainly (ii) but partly (iii).

b Janet's answer gives Frank a clear lead in framing his answer, but is not essential because he could have framed it to answer all the points more generally.

c Frank needs time to think of what he is going to say, and how he is going to say it.

Roleplay   Students could extend this conversation to give Frank's opinions, with Janet getting him to elaborate. See also: 'Getting and giving opinions', Unit B5.

2a Mr Conway understands fully. He is in a difficult position and needs time to think.

b No. This is a standard hesitation technique when faced with an embarrassing question.

c No, it isn't.

d Mr Conway needs to think how to word his explanation.

Roleplay   Enthusiastic students might enjoy extending this dialogue – defending Mr Conway's position and filling out Simon's arguments. See Unit B6 for agreeing and disagreeing, and Unit B9 for disapproving.

3a Henry's project is probably financially viable, but not obviously so.

b Yes, Mr Carter does know. Henry uses a long hesitant preamble before announcing that he has come to them as bankers.

c Mr Carter is basically doubtful about lending Henry money, and is leading up to telling him so.

d Mr Carter is not entirely in agreement with Henry.

e At the moment, Mr Carter probably won't lend the money.

f He first needs to check on Henry's current financial position.

Roleplay   This dialogue could be developed by students, with Mr Carter not willing to lend the money and Henry trying to persuade him.

Play the model exchanges on the cassette for the students to listen to, repeat and practise. Monitor for intonation, etc.

Exercise 1

Intonation notes

I'll have to think about that. Fall+rise. Fall on *think*. Rise on *that*.
How shall I put it? Usually mid-level.
That's a very interesting question. High-fall on *question*.
I'm glad you asked me that. Fall+rise. Fall on *glad*. Rise on *that*.
If you mean that . . . The continuation will have fall+rise.
I'm not quite sure what you mean by that. Low-fall.
I'm afraid I don't quite follow. Low-fall.
I quite see your point, but . . . Fall-rise on *point*.
Supplementary exercise Get students to provide written continuations of each phrase and then practise saying them aloud. Monitor for tone, appropriateness and effect.

Exercise 2

The choice of hesitation devices is arbitrary. Students should try to use a variety, as in the suggested responses.

Tapescript

1 Which country's popularity has remained unchanged between 1977 and 1983? (*Pause*)
   sr I'll have to think about that . . . It's Sweden.
2 Which country has decreased most in popularity since 1968? (*Pause*)
   sr That's a very interesting question . . . It's Switzerland.
3 Which country has continued to go up in popularity over the last fifteen years? (*Pause*)
   sr I'm glad you asked me that . . . It's Germany.
4 Which countries are more popular now than they were in 1968? (*Pause*)
   sr That's a very interesting question . . . There's only Germany.
5 How many countries are more popular now than they were in 1977? (*Pause*)
   sr I'll have to think about that . . . There are four.
6 Which countries gained in popularity between 1968 and 1977, but have declined between 1977 and 1983? (*Pause*)
   sr That's a very interesting question . . . Only France.
7 Which country do you think has gained most in popularity between 1977 and 1983? (*Pause*)
   sr I'm glad you asked me that . . . It's Germany.
8 Which country's popularity has remained most consistent during the whole period? (*Pause*)
   sr If you mean by that, which country has had more or less the same popularity all the time, then it's Italy.

Exercise 3

As with Exercise 2, the choice of hesitation devices is arbitrary and students should try to use a variety.

Tapescript

1 What percentage difference is there in the Swiss share of the market between 1973 and 1982? (*Pause*)
sr I'll have to think about that . . . The difference is 24 per cent.
2 How much has Japan's share of the market risen? (*Pause*)
sr That's a very interesting question . . . It's risen by 13 per cent.
3 How does the rise in Hongkong's share of the market compare with Japan's? (*Pause*)
sr I'm glad you asked me that . . . It has risen by the same amount.
4 Has any country's share of the market remained the same? (*Pause*)
sr I'll have to think about that . . . No, they have all changed.
5 Has any European country's share of the market gone up? (*Pause*)
sr I'll have to think about that . . . No, none.
6 Which of the two companies, SSIH and ASUAG, has made a bigger net loss over the period 1978–82? (*Pause*)
sr I'm glad you asked me that . . . It's ASUAG.
7 Which of the two seems to be doing better at the moment? (*Pause*)
sr If you mean by that, which one is losing less, then it's SSIH.
8 Which of the two has a higher turnover? (*Pause*)
sr That's a very interesting question . . . ASUAG has a higher turnover.

Exercise 4

There are no suggested responses – students to provide their own answers. Insist on the use of pause fillers.

Tapescript

1 Will the development of computers really give people the freedom to do more interesting tasks?
2 Will the benefits of the peaceful use of nuclear energy outweigh the military threat in the long run?
3 What would you say is the real function of international sport?
4 It's no longer possible for Third World countries to achieve full industrialisation, wouldn't you agree?
5 What would you say is the main purpose of education?
6 As water and air pollution is an international problem, how can it best be controlled?
7 How have ordinary people benefited from space research?
8 The money spent on space research would have been more useful spent on marine development, don't you think?

Exercise 5

Ask students to suggest variants on the phrases reviewed. Allow them to add acceptable variants to their books, unless they appear in Unit 1 of Section A or Section C.

Pairwork, groupwork and roleplay suggestions

No specific suggestions are given, since the need for hesitation devices will exist throughout Section B.

Unit 2 **Encounters, greetings and goodbyes, introductions**

Checkpoint

Notes for guidance

1a A business situation.

  b This question directs students to other formal or public situations where such phrases would be useful – at work, school, college, societies, clubs, etc.

2a This is a public introduction. Hamilton is going to speak or demonstrate something to a group of people who have met for that purpose.

  b He may be genuinely pleased to be there, but the point is that this is a standard way of starting a public speech or demonstration whether you are pleased to be there or not.

3a A self-introduction.

  b Students will need it whenever explaining their presence to someone, or in a situation where they are not expected or not known.

4a Justin's is also a self-introduction, the difference being that he is expected; he has an appointment. He therefore gives no apology for the disturbance. He does thank Mr Jones for seeing him at short notice, though. Check understanding of this phrase.

  b This conversation probably takes place in an office or a bank. Note that Justin's last phrase, *The thing is . . .* warns Mr Jones that he has a problem to discuss.

5 David's terminology and register suggest he is concluding a report to a committee of businessmen, or of a club or society. He would therefore appear to be treasurer or financial director. His final sentence indicates that he has been talking for some time.

6a The most likely explanation is that Linda has put Fred up for a few days.

  b He is therefore thanking her for her hospitality.

  c He may or may not want her to visit him. Once again this is a standard social formula, used when giving thanks for hospitality and making an offer to reciprocate.

Play the model exchanges on the cassette for the students to listen to, repeat and practise. Monitor for intonation, etc.

Exercise 1

Names are given in initial introduction phrases for ease of repetition and practice. The same names can be used throughout, or students' names can be substituted.

Supplementary exercise Get students to provide written continuations of each phrase and then practise saying them aloud. Monitor for tone, appropriateness and effect.

Exercise 2

Suggested answers are as in the tapescript for Exercise 3. Any deviant responses should be examined for differences in tone, appropriateness and effect.

Exercise 3

Remember to pause the cassette recorder to give students time to respond.

Tapescript

1 A famous teacher has agreed to give a lecture to your English class.
   Introduce him to the other students. (*Pause*)
   SR We're very fortunate to have with us today Mr Carter, who is going to talk to us on the very interesting subject . . .
2 A friend has just arrived from the USA. Introduce her to your boss. (*Pause*)
   SR I'd like to introduce you to Sheila Black, Mr Whitman.
3 You arrive at the dentist's for your six-monthly examination. (*Pause*)
   SR Good morning. My name's Brian Drinkwater. I've got an appointment with Mr Lamb.
4 You're in a big office block, trying to find Miss Page's office. You see a secretary typing. (*Pause*)
   SR Excuse me, I'm sorry to trouble you. My name's Forbes, I'm looking for Miss Page's office.
5 You're introduced to your favourite writer, Nigel Thomas, at a cocktail party. (*Pause*)
   SR It's a very great pleasure to meet you, Mr Thomas.
6 You're saying goodbye to your host family after a pleasant stay in London. (*Pause*)
   SR Thank you so much for everything. And do come and see me when you're in my own . . .
7 You've arranged to see your doctor to get a vaccination certificate you need urgently. You're shown into his office. (*Pause*)
   SR Good morning, Dr Brown. Thank you for seeing me at such short notice.
8 You're just beginning your talk on life in your home town to a group of foreign students. (*Pause*)
   SR I'm very pleased to be here today to talk to you about life in my home town. I come from . . .

Notes on the tapescript

1 A degree of public voice projection is implied in this situation, as the sr demonstrates.
2 The sr gives a direct, standard, polite introduction. Ask students to elaborate and develop similar introductions at the end of this exercise.
3 This is a standard self-introduction in a public situation: salutation; self-introduction; announcement of reason for arrival.
   At the end of the exercise ask students to announce themselves in similar situations.
4 The first sentence is to attract the secretary's attention, and uses the upper part of the voice range. The implied question in the second sentence requires use of a fall+rise nucleus on _Page's._
5 Sincerity is demonstrated by high-head with an emphatic stress on _very_ and high-fall nucleus on _meet._
6 The first sentence has emphatic stepping-head, high-fall nucleus on _everything._ The second sentence has high-fall nucleus on _do_, low tail. Slightly artificial elaborate forms are used here, so use the upper part of the voice range.
7 This is another public, elaborate form of self-introduction, but this situation requires less emphatic delivery.
8 In contrast, this response requires public voice projection.

Exercise 4

Remind students to speak when they hear the beep. Pause the cassette recorder to give students time to respond to the situation described before listening to the suggested response.

Tapescript

1 A Ah, there you are! I don't believe you've met Dr Cooper from Canada, have you? (*Beep*)
  SR Ah no, I haven't. It's a very great pleasure to meet you.
2 A I've been looking forward to this talk for months – tonight's speaker is the best man in the field, you know.
  B Really? What's his name?
  A Oh, er, it's Burgess, I think. Oh, but never mind, here he comes now. The Chairman's going to introduce him, I think. (*Beep*)
  SR Good evening, ladies and gentlemen, we're very fortunate to have with us this evening Mr Burgess, who is the Director of the International Institute in New South Wales.
3 A Has the person arrived to see Mr Poole yet, Nancy? He was due here at 11 o'clock.
  B No, I don't think so – oh look, though, someone's coming now. He looks in a hurry. (*Beep*)

SR Oh, good morning. My name's Philips. I've got an appointment with Mr Poole at 11 o'clock.

4 A Come this way, please. The manager will see you now. You're quite lucky he could see you so quickly, you know. He's very busy today. (*Knocks*)

B Oh, hello. Do come in. What can I do for you? (*Beep*)

SR Well, er, thank you very much for seeing me at such short notice. The thing is . . .

5 A I've really enjoyed our little talk, and, as I said, I plan to be back in your lovely country some time next year on another business trip. (*Beep*)

SR Well, it's been very nice meeting you. I hope to meet you again when you're next here.

6 A Oh do please stay! We need your help and advice. (*Beep*)

SR I'm sorry I can't stay any longer. I have an appointment later this afternoon and I have to . . .

Notes on the tapescript

1 An acceptable variant would be *No, I haven't. How do you do?* but the SR expresses greater warmth towards the foreign visitor.

2 The dialogue before the beep conveys the information needed for the SR. However, this is quite a complicated situation. Suggest you play the prompt dialogue twice before students respond. Obviously Mr Burgess can be introduced as representing any appropriate institution or organisation. Check for students' public voice projection.

3 Again, sufficient information is given to elicit the self-introduction of an expected, but late visitor. Repeat and practise this exchange at the end of the exercise.

4 Repeats the *thank you for seeing me* situation in Exercise 3. B's speech indicates that he knows the caller, so no self-introduction is necessary. Thus the caller should tell him what the problem is briefly and without delay. The SR demonstrates slight hesitation; thanks for B's agreeing to see him; and introduction of the problem. Check for all these in students' variants.

6 An apology for leaving is followed by an explanation in the face of an emphatic request not to leave. Ask students to think of a continuation of this exchange at the end of the complete exercise, and to practise it as a roleplay in pairs.

Exercise 5

Ask students to suggest variants on the phrases reviewed. Allow them to enter them in their books, unless they appear in Unit 6 of Section A or Section B.

Unit 3 **Information gathering**

Checkpoint

Notes for guidance

1a The exchange takes place in a secretary's office, in this case in a bank. Mr Carter is the bank manager.

  b Beatrice is Brian Carter's secretary. David is a client of the bank.

  c David says this because he wants to put forward a question he has already asked, but in a slightly different form.

  d Beatrice probably wouldn't have agreed to find out by this afternoon.

2a No, Richard doesn't know Simon.

  b The conversation is probably taking place in a pub, café, or maybe a railway carriage.

  c It is too personal a question to ask (about the cost of someone else's property) without prefacing it in this manner.

  d Probably, Simon was going to say that he got it at trade price, or perhaps that it doesn't belong to him and so he doesn't know the price.

  e Richard probably thinks that Simon was going to say that he doesn't know because the camera doesn't belong to him.

Roleplay This conversation could be continued. How would it go on?

3a Brian probably knows Henry Wyatt pretty well.

  b Brian is a bank manager. Henry's company has its account at Brian's bank.

  c Brian wishes to clarify the position, but doesn't want to sound aggressive.

  d Brian would have sounded aggressive. Henry would be hostile and defensive, and it would be more difficult to find a solution to the situation.

Roleplay Again this dialogue could be extended by imaginative students, with Henry defending a difficult position against the demands of the bank manager.

Play the model exchanges on the cassette for the students to listen to, repeat and practise. Monitor for intonation, etc.

Exercise 1

The phrases in this unit would all be uttered in the upper part of the voice range so as not to sound impolite. Note that, *I think I'm right in saying . . . aren't I?* requires a rising question tag.

Supplementary exercise Get students to provide written continuations of each phrase and then practise saying them aloud. Monitor for tone, appropriateness and effect.

Exercise 2

Suggested answers are as in the tapescript for Exercise 3. Any deviant responses should be examined for differences in tone, appropriateness and effect.

Exercise 3

Remember to pause the cassette recorder to give students time to respond.

Tapescript

DAVID Thank you very much for seeing me at such short notice. (*Beep*)

1 BRIAN Am I right in thinking that you would like to borrow £3000?

DAVID Yes, that's right, £3000. (*Beep*)

2 BRIAN Would I be right in saying that you wish to buy a new car?

DAVID Yes, that's right. I'm afraid my old one is getting too unreliable. (*Beep*)

3 BRIAN I hope you don't mind my asking, but what sort of car are you thinking of buying?

DAVID Not at all – a British Leyland Maestro. (*Beep*)

4 BRIAN Perhaps you could tell me if you want to buy a new or a second-hand car.

DAVID Oh, a second-hand one. I don't think I can afford a new one. (*Beep*)

5 BRIAN Might I ask if you have a particular car in mind?

DAVID Well, as a matter of fact I have, yes. (*Beep*)

6 BRIAN And if I might just ask, how old is it?

DAVID Um . . . it's one year old – only done five thousand miles. (*Beep*)

7 BRIAN Would I be right in saying that you intend to put £2000 towards it yourself?

DAVID Er yes . . . er . . . £2000. (*Beep*)

8 BRIAN And I think I'm right in saying that you would like to repay over two years, aren't I?

DAVID Yes, that's right – that is if it would be all right with you.

BRIAN Well, I think it probably will be. If you would care to fill in this form, we'll deal with the application as fast as we can.

DAVID Thank you very much.

Notes on the tapescript

3 The make of the car is not entirely relevant to whether the loan is granted or not, hence the form of the question.

4 This is more relevant to the granting of a loan. This is information Brian needs to have.

5 and 6 This is further information that Brian would need to have.

The other questions are to check the information that Brian would already have been given before agreeing to see David.

Exercise 4

Tapescript

1 You have been looking for a copy of a certain book for some time. You see someone you don't know who has one. Ask him where he got it. (*Pause*)
sʀ I hope you don't mind my asking, but could you tell me where you got that book?

2 You want to know how much it cost. (*Pause*)
sʀ Would you mind if I asked how much it cost?

3 You are at a directors' meeting. A colleague says, Sales have suffered somewhat. You <u>think</u> she means they have fallen sharply. Ask her to clarify. (*Pause*)
sʀ When you say that sales have suffered somewhat, do you mean that they have fallen sharply?

4 You are in the chair at a board meeting. A member of the board has just mentioned the possible influence of the fluctuation in exchange rates on the business. Ask Frank, the financial director, to state how the rates have changed. (*Pause*)
sʀ Perhaps Frank would like to tell us exactly how the exchange rates have changed.

5 You are a company manager. Your secretary has told you that one of your employees would like some time off without pay. Check with the employee. (*Pause*)
sʀ Am I right in thinking you would like some time off without pay?

6 Find out from the employee how much time off she wants. (*Pause*)
sʀ Might I ask how much time off you want?

7 It's a slightly personal question, but you need to know why she wants the time off. (*Pause*)
sʀ I hope you don't mind my asking, but why do you need this time off?

8 In fact she is getting married. Now for a truly personal question. You are interested to know how long they have known each other. (*Pause*)
sʀ I know it's a personal question, but would you mind if I asked how long you have known each other?

Notes on the tapescript

1 This is a request for specific information from a stranger.
2 This is a follow-up question to no. 1.
3 This clarifies what someone has just said.
4 This introduces another speaker into the discussion.
5 You are checking your information.
6 This is a follow-up question to no. 5, a more personal question.
7 This is another personal question. Is it really necessary to know?
8 This is a very personal question. This has nothing to do with whether or not you agree to give her time off.

Exercise 5

Ask students to suggest variants on the phrases reviewed. Allow them to add acceptable variants to their books, unless they appear in Unit 3 of Section A or Section C.

Pairwork, groupwork and roleplay suggestions

1 Interview for a job. See 'Giving information' in Unit B4.
2 Policeman interviewing a witness. See Unit C4.
3 Journalist interviewing a member of the public or a politician. See 'Giving information' in Unit C4.

Unit 4 **Giving information and instructions**

Checkpoint

Notes for guidance

1 This is a meeting of local residents to discuss what should be done about a proposed road development scheme.
2 Richard is interrupted all the time because what he is saying is rambling, and the other people have no clear sense of any contribution being made to the discussion.
3 Justin is trying to interrupt Richard in the middle of a sentence.
4 Richard wishes to prevent Justin's interruption.
5 It is rude to interrupt someone who is speaking, so it is necessary to apologise and announce one's intention to interrupt. This is a standard phrase.
6 Richard doesn't stop David because David interrupted at the end of the point that Richard was making.
7 By announcing that he has two points to make, Frank assures himself of the attention of the listeners while he makes them.
8 By enumerating them and saying *Firstly*, he makes it difficult to interrupt, as the listeners know that there is a second point that they must wait for. See note 7.
9 Both David and Frank, unlike Richard, announce clearly that they have a contribution to make to the discussion, and therefore they are heard out without interruption until they have put forward their points of view.

Roleplay This discussion could be extended with the same people elaborating their positions, and others coming in. Alternatively it could be used as a starting point for a general discussion on traffic and pollution, traffic and the environment, conservation of natural resources and development on other related topics. Techniques also involved are: giving and getting opinions (Units A5 and B5); agreeing and disagreeing (Units A6 and B6).

Play the model exchanges on the cassette for the students to listen to, repeat and practise. Monitor for intonation, etc.

Exercise 1

There are no intonation problems to highlight.
Supplementary exercise Get students to provide written continuations of each phrase and then practise saying them aloud. Monitor for tone, appropriateness and effect.

Exercise 2

Suggested answers are as in the tapescript for Exercise 3. Any deviant responses should be examined for differences in tone, appropriateness and effect.

Exercise 3

Remember to pause the cassette recorder to give students time to respond.

Tapescript (a)

CUSTOMER Good morning. I'm interested in buying a typewriter. Could you possibly tell me something about this machine please? (*Pause*)
SR First of all, can I say that this typewriter has all the latest features.
CUSTOMER Ah, that sounds very interesting. (*Pause*)
SR Firstly, it has computer interface connectability.
CUSTOMER Yes, that is very useful. (*Pause*)
SR Secondly, it has the advanced daisy-wheel print-head.
CUSTOMER Oh good, I was going to ask about that. (*Pause*)
SR Thirdly, it has lift-off correction with one-line memory.
CUSTOMER Ah, that's a very good point. That only leaves the small matter of the cost. How much?

Tapescript (b)

SALESMAN Good morning. I hope I can interest you in our latest typewriter, the BM 6021. First of all, can I say that this typewriter has all the latest features. (*Beep*)
MANAGER Before you go on, I must tell you that all our typewriters already have all the latest features.
SALESMAN As I was saying, it has all the latest features. Firstly, it has computer interface connectability. (*Beep*)
MANAGER I'm sorry to break in, but I ought to point out that all our typewriters already have computer interface connectability.
SALESMAN Yes . . . well . . . Secondly, I must tell you that it has the advanced daisy-wheel print-head. (*Beep*)
MANAGER I don't want to interrupt, but can I just say that all our typewriters already have the advanced daisy wheel print-head.
SALESMAN I see . . . er . . . yes . . . and . . . well thirdly, let me add that it has lift-off correction with one-line memory. (*Beep*)
MANAGER I must stop you to say that all our typewriters already have lift-off correction with one-line memory.
SALESMAN Oh . . . I see . . . yes, well . . . in that case . . . er . . . perhaps . . .

Notes on the tapescripts

The same material is used in the two parts of this exercise, firstly in an information ordering function, and then as a basis for an interrupting function.

In the first part, the order in the suggested responses is the one we feel to be natural, with global feature before detail and then going from most advanced to least advanced. Students should be encouraged to try to work out their own presentation order – not just taking the sequence of visual prompts, which are random and un-numbered.

In the second part, the choice of which interruption phrase to use at which point is essentially arbitrary, though we think that the first and the last, as given on the tape, are in their natural positions.

In these responses, the intonation nucleus should be on *have* – a high-fall.

Exercise 4

In this exercise there is a beep to signal where to pause the tape, as in some cases students are required to interrupt in the middle of a sentence.

Tapescript

1 In view of the way that the pound has increased in value against other world currencies so consistently over the past few years, . . . er . . . (*Beep*)
sr I'm sorry to break in, but it hasn't increased in value against the other world currencies!

2 I wonder whether production in home computers won't always far outstrip demand, even in the West. But perhaps you know more about that? (*Beep*)
sr Well, I must tell you that, in fact, demand already far outstrips production.

3 The market for home computers is absolutely flooded, so I don't think there's much point in investing in the development of a new one. (*Beep*)
sr Before you go on, can I say that the market is far from flooded.

4 So, of course, since Great Britain will never have a woman Prime Minister, . . . er . . . (*Beep*)
sr I don't want to interrupt, but I must point out that Britain already has a woman Prime Minister.

5 I'm sorry. I didn't quite follow what you were saying about learning English and its being widely spoken. (*Beep*)
sr Well, what I meant to say was that it's very important to learn English as it is spoken more widely than any other language.

6 And . . . er . . . well . . . as only to be expected . . . er . . . there is such a lot of agreement between East and West on all things . . . er . . . (*Beep*)
sr I must stop you to point out that in fact there is hardly any agreement between East and West!

7 Of course, the reason the Americans want to build the first permanent space station is that the Russians were the first to put a man on the Moon, and . . . er . . . (*Beep*)
sr I don't want to break in, but I must point out that it was the Americans who put the first man on the Moon.

8 You were saying something about small cars being better in cities because of . . . was it parking, and something else . . . ? (*Beep*) sʀ Yes. Well there are two points I'd like to make. Firstly, it's much easier to park a small car in a city, and, secondly, they use less fuel in traffic.

Notes on the tapescript

1 This is a mid-sentence interruption. The intonation nucleus is high-fall on *hasn't*.

2 *I would like to point out that*, or *I ought to point out that*, would be suitable alternative presenting phrases. The other speaker is contradicted. Fall-rise on *demand*. High-fall on *production*.

3 You are contradicting here at a break in the other person's speech, so this is the most suitable interruption phrase. High-fall nucleus on *far*.

4 This is interrupting in the middle of a sentence. High-fall nucleus on *has*.

5 This rephrases information.

6 This interrupts in mid-sentence. Nucleus, high-fall on *any*.

7 This is a mid-sentence interruption. High-fall nucleus on *Americans*.

8 The prompt requires two points of information, so we use this presentation and enumeration.

Exercise 5

Ask students to suggest variants on the phrases reviewed. Allow them to add acceptable variants in their books, unless they appear in Unit 4 of Section A or Section C.

Pairwork, groupwork and roleplay suggestions

Information presentation: Salesman presenting other types of equipment. Any business presentation situation.
Interruption techniques: Any group discussion of a subject of general interest.

Unit 5 **Getting and giving opinions**

Checkpoint

Notes for guidance

1a Bertram employs a common indirect form to ask for an opinion. *What do you think about . . .?*, being far more direct, implies far greater excitement and greater urgency.

  b The second question draws attention to the use of *quite* as *absolutely*: Sidney disagrees with most of the professor's article completely.

Roleplay   Ask students to continue this exchange as Bertram and Sidney, then as themselves in pairs.

2 The elaborate forms employed suggest that this is a TV interview.
Roleplay   Ask students to continue this interview in the same characters.

3 Questions draw students' attention to the use of this tense as an <u>indirect</u> approach to asking a question. Miss Watkins is therefore probably senior in age or status to Linda, who approaches her slightly hesitantly.
Roleplay   Students to invent parallel situations and employ the present perfect continuous form to elicit opinions. Monitor for effectiveness of request, and appropriateness of the opinions given.

4a Philip feels very strongly, hence his *I'm absolutely convinced . . .*

  b Robert employs a common technique for interrupting in a public or formal situation. His apology is a convention for breaking into another's speech, and he could continue speaking until he in turn is interrupted.

  c Roland probably foresaw that this issue would arouse controversy, hence his, *Do you hold any strong views on that?*

Roleplay   Ask students to work in threes and continue this exchange with the same characters.

5a No. By asking what George's *position* (not *opinion*) is, Henry is clearly seeking a public stance, not an emotional response.

  b George responds by giving an impersonal opinion – that of his department, emphasised by the use of *we*.

  c The interruption is shorter; the speaker only wants to interject one piece of information and not to take over the conversation, hence the beginning, *Could I just say . . .* Notice the further elaborate form of George's second speech.

6 The phrase <u>not</u> mentioned is, once again, *In my opinion . . .* It has been omitted, and attention drawn to the fact, in order to show that it is a phrase more taught than used in both formal and everyday speech. More natural phrases are to be preferred.

Exercise 1

Supplementary exercise   Get students to provide written continuations of each phrase and then practise saying them aloud. Monitor for tone, appropriateness and effect.

Exercise 2

Suggested answers are as in the tapescript for Exercise 3. Any deviant responses should be examined for differences in tone, appropriateness and effect.

Exercise 3

Remember to pause the cassette recorder to give students time to respond. They should speak after the beep.

Tapescript

1 MD Ah, there you are. Do come in. Now what did you want to see me about? (*Beep*)
   SR I was wondering what you thought about my last report.

2 COMMITTEE MEMBER Well, I don't know whether we really need these facilities at all. What do you feel about that? (*Beep*)
   SR There's no doubt in my mind that these facilities are absolutely essential.

3 CHAIRMAN I wonder what the representative of the Electrical Department of our Ruritanian factory thinks about the general level of efficiency in his plant? (*Beep*)
   SR Well, as far as my department's concerned, efficiency is already of a very high order. Some of the other departments, though, are at a somewhat less advanced . . .

4 COMMITTEE MEMBER I'm interested to know who we all think should be the treasurer on next year's committee. (*Beep*)
   SR I'm sure you'll all agree when I say that Maria is the obvious choice for this post. After all, she was treasurer last year, and I know we all . . .

5 BUSINESSMAN . . . Well that's sorted that problem out. Now, are there any other subjects we need to discuss before you go? (*Beep*)
   SR Well, I've been meaning to ask you for your opinion on the modernisation proposals.

6 STUDENT . . . and so for all these reasons I'm convinced that English has no place as a world language in the modern world . . . (*Beep*)
   SR Look, I'm sorry, I don't want to interrupt, but I do feel you're quite wrong on this particular point.

7 INTERVIEWER A lot of people are very worried about the so-called disappearing whale. Now, do you honestly think that the whale will become extinct in the next few years? (*Beep*)

sr I think it's certainly true to say that their numbers have been greatly reduced over the last fifty years. Nevertheless I don't feel that there is any immediate danger of their becoming completely extinct, as . . .

8 SPEAKER . . . and I simply feel that the one quality so sadly missing in world affairs is tolerance. Tolerance of other people's views or other countries' customs or whatever. (*Beep*)

sr Hear, hear.

Notes on the tapescript

1 Check that students are using the upper part of the voice range, reflecting hesitant enquiry.

2 Check for evenly stressed, forceful, convinced delivery.

3 sr revises the impersonal opinion. Hence a reasonable tone is required.

4 Assumption of group agreement is here used as a way of selling an opinion – of persuading, in fact. But the element of bluff in this technique requires a straightforward, even delivery; no undue emphasis is needed on *agree, Maria* or *obvious*.

5 sr shows introduction of a new topic – a request for an opinion – with some slight hesitation, and revises the *I was wondering . . .* technique.

6 Interruption technique is practised here. sr disagrees firmly – *Look . . . I do feel you're quite wrong . . .* – and apologises for breaking in on the speaker's flow.

7 The situation implies that an expert is being interviewed, and is giving a balanced view on a problem. Therefore, the response is in two halves. In the first sentence there is a high-fall nucleus on *reduced*. This is balanced in the second sentence by the nuclear stress on *extinct*. The tone as a whole should reflect a balanced judgement, neither excited nor bored.

8 The interruption is in favour of the speaker's opinion, and should therefore convey enthusiasm and brief support.

Exercise 4

Pause the tape after the beep to give students time to respond.

Tapescript

1 You want to know what your business colleague thinks of the latest sales figures, published last month. You say: (*Beep*)

sr I've been meaning to ask you what you thought about the latest sales figures.

2 You submitted plans to your head teacher for an improved timetable for next year. Two weeks later you are talking to him at coffee time and want to find out what he thinks of your plans. You say: (*Beep*)

sr I was wondering what you thought about my plans for the timetable for next year, sir?

3 You are interviewing Mr Brown, the leader of a conservationist group, for your local newspaper. You want to know if his organisation agrees with unlawful demonstrations to make its point more widely known. You say: (*Beep*)

sr What is your position with regard to unlawful demonstrations, Mr Brown?

In the next three questions you have to give an opinion in various situations. Remember that the way you give your opinion is just as important as the opinion itself – at least for this exercise!

4 You're at a business meeting and are trying to get your colleagues to concentrate on increasing sales. Other points of view are that new products should be developed and that efficiency should be increased. You're asked for your opinion. You say: (*Beep*)

sr Wouldn't you all agree that increasing sales has to be our first priority? I mean, without good sales there's no point in the other priorities, is there?

5 You're absolutely sure that the latest Sankey hi-fi system is the best on the market. You're asked if you prefer it to the previous Sankey model. You say: (*Beep*)

sr There's no doubt in my mind that the latest model is the better of the two. In fact, I would say that it's the best on the market at the moment.

6 You're representing your college at an international convention and are asked your opinion on joining a multinational swimming competition. You love the idea, but not many people at your college like swimming. You say: (*Beep*)

sr Well, as far as I'm concerned, I think it would be an excellent idea, but I'm not sure that the other members of my college would be keen on joining in.

In the last two questions you have to interrupt someone with a suitable phrase and in a suitable manner! The beep will tell you when to speak.

7 You disagree strongly with the point of view being expressed by your colleague, Frank, but he obviously wants to continue his line of argument. (*Beep*)

sr I'm sorry, Frank, I don't want to interrupt, but I'm afraid I don't agree with your point of view at all.

8 You are the chairman of a business discussion which is most interesting, but you notice that the time is now ten past one and you were all due at a restaurant for lunch at one o'clock. You have to interrupt the speakers to tell them this. You say: (*Beep*)

sr Ladies and gentlemen, could I just interrupt to say that it's now ten past one, and interesting though this discussion is, we were supposed to be at the restaurant at one, so I think we'd better adjourn and maybe continue our discussion over lunch.

Notes on the tapescript

1 The alternative indirect form, using the present perfect continuous, was chosen because it does not imply the same degree of hesitancy as is needed for No. 2.
2 This returns to the *I was wondering . . .* form. The speaker uses greater hesitancy when talking to a superior.
3 A formal interview situation provokes elaborate forms: *What is your position . . . ?* not *What do you think . . . ?*; *with regard to* not *about*. Students' variants should demonstrate an awareness of the necessity for such forms in this context.
4 A problem situation calls for students to attempt to unite others in agreement. sʀ introduces a technique for doing this, and a reason for hoping all can agree. Students' variants should be compared with this.
5 Firmness of belief is conveyed in the sʀ by *no doubt in my mind . . .* and *in fact*. Students' intonation should convey similar conviction without aggression.
6 The sʀ's first section limits opinion to the speaker's belief; the second section goes on to give the reservations of others. Students' variants should contain these two elements: personal agreement and expression of others' disagreement.
7 The sʀ revises interrupting and stopping another in order to voice a contradictory opinion. After the exercise, students can be asked to continue and extend this exchange in paired roleplay.
8 The situation calls for an interruption for a specific purpose – to bring a new piece of information to the attention of the group. Public voice projection is called for, but with good humour, not aggression.

Exercise 5

Ask students to suggest variants on the phrases reviewed. Allow them to add acceptable variants to their books, unless they appear in Unit 5 of Section A or Section C.

Pairwork, groupwork and roleplay suggestions

Refer back to the students' written continuations of the phrases in Exercise 1 (supplementary exercise). In the light of subsequent practice (Exercises 2, 3, 4, 5), ask them to use these monitored sentences as the basis for conversation in pairs or groups, extending or developing their original ideas.

Unit 6 **Agreeing and disagreeing**

Checkpoint

Notes for guidance

1 The area of language, e.g. *level of productivity* and *competitive in this field*, indicates a business setting. *Finally* indicates a speech of some length. The exchange therefore is probably at a board meeting of a company. David's response signifies complete and public assent.

2 They could be friends or fellow students. Joanna's certainty of opinion and Justin's complete agreement suggest that she is by far the stronger character of the two, which could lead to the assumption of a teacher–pupil relationship.

3a Desmond's response is a formula for agreeing publicly with another's opinion.

 b However, by adding *most of what you said* and then *Nevertheless*, Desmond is signalling that he intends to disagree with certain parts of William's opinions, perhaps forcibly. He therefore tries to minimise the threat of this disagreement by expressing happiness at being able to agree in part.

Roleplay Ask students to extend this exchange – forwards and backwards – in the characters of William and Desmond.

4 Frank progresses from voicing a perfectly acceptable explanation of his problem to a somewhat extreme remedy for it. Simon therefore changes from complete agreement to an expression of reserved disagreement. The nucleus in his second statement would fall naturally on the final *that*.

Roleplay Ask students to continue this exchange as Frank and Simon, suggesting different solutions for the football club's problems, with corresponding agreements and disagreements.

5a Beatrice is extremely direct in giving her opinion – to the point of pomposity.

 b Shirley's disagreement is firm but contained. She expresses regret before rejecting Beatrice's opinion.

Roleplay Ask students to continue this discussion. Monitor closely and check how long this type of argument can continue before either becoming a shouting match or collapsing altogether. Ask students what they can deduce from such an approach to agreeing and disagreeing in public.

Play the model exchanges on the cassette for students to listen to, repeat and practise. Monitor for intonation, etc.

Exercise 1

Phrases begin with complete agreement, and progress through qualified agreement and qualified disagreement to complete disagreement.
Supplementary exercise   Get students to provide written continuation of each phrase and then practise saying them aloud. Monitor for tone, appropriateness and effect.

Exercise 2

Suggested answers are as in the tapescript for Exercise 3. Any deviant responses should be examined for differences in tone, appropriateness and effect.

Exercise 3

Remember to pause the cassette recorder to give students time to respond.

Tapescript

1 There's no doubt we're over the worst of the world recession. (*Pause*)
   sr Yes, I'm in total agreement with that point of view.
2 The main point of studying English is to get an academic qualification. (*Pause*)
   sr I'm sorry, but I really can't agree with you on that.
3 . . . and my conclusion is that by the end of the decade all teaching will be done by computer. (*Pause*)
   sr Although most of what you said is perfectly acceptable, I don't think I can agree with you on your point about all teaching being done by computer.
4 So as the world's resources of coal and oil will undoubtedly be exhausted by the end of the century, there's clearly no doubt that nuclear power holds the one key to the future. (*Pause*)
   sr I don't think I'd put it quite as strongly as that.
5 Don't you agree that the more a student enjoys his studies, the more he will benefit from them? (*Pause*)
   sr Yes, I agree one hundred per cent.
6 In the modern world the business that is not efficient is doomed to failure . . . (*Pause*)
   sr I entirely agree.
7 . . . and to be efficient a company must be able to sell its products in the language of its potential customers. (*Pause*)
   sr I totally agree with everything you've said.
8 It's a sad but true fact that people over thirty-five will never really understand how to get on with computers. (*Pause*)
   sr Well, I'm not sure I agree with you on that.

Notes on the tapescript

Obviously no one can predict student opinions. The responses chosen are considered to be the most likely.

1 This is possibly the most controversial of the eight exchanges. Nevertheless the sr corresponds to a common belief, and the intonation should demonstrate confidence and enthusiasm in agreement.

2 A misguided opinion should provoke apologetic disagreement. High-head on *sorry*, with accents on _really_ and *agree*. High-fall nucleus on *that*.

3 An unlikely assumption evinces qualified rejection. Point out how one can disagree with a specific item without rejecting all of another person's opinions. Also practise *I don't think I can agree with you on your point about . . .*; a firm but discreet disagreement form.

4 The speaker overstates her case: *the one key* provoking disagreement in degree. There is a falling head. Fall-rise nucleus on *that*.

5 An unexceptionable opinion should gain complete agreement. sr should show enthusiasm.

6 The key word, *entirely*, produces a contrasting intonation pattern: low pre-head, high-fall nucleus on _entirely_; low-level tail.

7 and 8 The total agreement in (7) contrasts with qualified disagreement in (8).

Exercise 4

Tapescript

1 I'm afraid the career you've chosen for yourself offers very little scope for promotion.
   Disagree firmly. (*Pause*)
   sr I'm sorry, but I really can't agree with you on that.

2 There's no doubt that unemployment is going to get worse, not better. And therefore more people will have more leisure time. It's therefore imperative that people should be educated to fill their leisure time constructively.
   Agree completely with everything that has been said. (*Pause*)
   sr I'm in total accord with everything that has been said.

3 Wouldn't you agree that we're living through a period of radical change in employment patterns, arising from computerisation, automation and so on . . . ?
   Agree firmly. (*Pause*)
   sr Yes, I agree with you one hundred per cent.

4 The trouble with modern classical composers is that they write for other musicians, not the general public. It follows that the only music of today which will be of interest to future generations is pop music.
   Disagree with part of this point of view. (*Pause*)
   sr Although most of what you've said is perfectly acceptable, I don't think I

can agree with you that the <u>only</u> music which will be of interest is pop music.

5 Let's face facts. In the modern world sport <u>is</u> political. So it's only sensible to make the best political use of it we can.
    Disagree politely but firmly. (*Pause*)
    sr I'm sorry, but I really can't agree with you on that.

6 Obviously, constitutional monarchy is the only system of government which guarantees the freedom of the people.
    You think the speaker is overstating his case. (*Pause*)
    sr I don't think I'd put it quite as strongly as that.

7 Trade unions would do well to remember that their responsibility to society as a whole is greater than their responsibility to their members.
    Disagree totally with that standpoint. (*Pause*)
    sr I'm afraid I totally reject that point of view.

8 The golden age of the cinema is well and truly over. There are no great films being made any more.
    You haven't yet decided what you think about this – but you know you've seen some very good films recently. (*Pause*)
    sr I'm not sure I agree with you on that.

Notes on the tapescript

1 The firmness of disagreement required does not preclude apologising for the disagreement or the use of *can't* or *don't*.

2 The elaborate language of the prompt is designed to provoke a formal response. Hence the sr uses *total accord*, followed by the passive mood to indicate public agreement.

3 Several variants are possible. All should be introduced by *Yes*, with a direct reply.

4 This revises disagreeing with part of someone's point of view. Student variants should encompass this distinction within the area of formal disagreement.

5 This is a blunt expression of a blunt opinion. sr shows firm but polite disagreement, taking the heat out of the exchange but also attempting to stop further discussion of the point.

6 sr revises modifying a disagreement phrase. Discuss this form again at the end of the whole exercise.

7 sr revises a disagreeing form from the model exchanges: public rejection of another's viewpoint. Contrast with No. 8.

8 This is a less positive disagreement phrase; partially a hesitation device for buying time while thinking of counter arguments.

Exercise 5

Ask students to suggest variants on the phrases reviewed. Allow them to add acceptable variants to their books, unless they appear in Unit 6 of Section A or Section C.

Pairwork, groupwork and roleplay suggestions

Refer back to the students' written continuations of the phrases in
Exercise 1 (supplementary exercise). In the light of subsequent practice
(Exercises 2, 3, 4, 5), ask them to use these monitored sentences as the
basis for conversation in pairs or groups, extending or developing
their original ideas.

Unit 7 Getting what you want, making requests, giving and refusing permission

Checkpoint

Notes for guidance

1   David's request form, *I wonder if you could*, indicates that Frank could be his senior, an impression reinforced by Frank's *Come on up*.

2a The first question is to check correct understanding of the *Would you mind . . . -ing me?* construction. Variants have to be re-phrased: *Could you possibly give me . . . ?*, etc. An indirect request is needed, as Joanna has herself caused the problem.
  b The receptionist may be perfectly genuine in her expression of regret; her tone at any rate will suggest that she is (see apologies in Units A10 and B10).

3a The first question checks and tests students' understanding of the *Would you mind if . . .?* construction. A variant would be, *Could I possibly . . . ?* or *Is it all right with you if . . . ?*, but neither fits the situation as well. A direct translation of *Would you mind . . . ?* is *Would it be a problem for you . . . ?*, but this is clumsy and rarely used.
  b Arthur uses indirect refusal forms to distance his own feelings from his professional refusal, but it is impossible to tell if he personally dislikes Keith's suggestion.
  c Keith then employs a request ending with *I'd be very grateful* – a common second line of attack request.
  d Arthur then goes further in distancing his personal inclinations from his public refusal; he softens his mode of refusal while refusing to change or reconsider that refusal.
  e In their final exchange, Keith modifies his request sufficiently for Arthur to be able to give his official seal of approval.

4a Requesting elements: *I know it's not a good time to talk to you, but . . .; I was wondering if . . .; . . . you see and . . .*
  b Cartwright is totally unsympathetic and employs the barest minimum of regret in his refusal. Willis's attempt at persuasion only provokes a further blunt rejection.

5a Henry's request is barely polite; a more direct order would provoke a hostile reaction.
  b He is not <u>more</u> polite, as presumably he is fairly irate at finding his driveway blocked by Justin!

6a The exchange could possibly be at a job interview, although Sally's reply suggests that she is about to embark on her whole life story.

b Her *I'd be delighted to* is very much a social formula – as much a time-gaining device as a request acceptance, and first cousin to the politician's *That's a very good question.*

7a No, in both cases. Both are examples of cold British politeness, which contains but often does not conceal irritation or annoyance. The *Would you be so kind as to . . . ?* form, in particular, is used to convey an icy command in the garb of social correctness.

b Also, the apparent casualness of *I'd rather not, actually* masks a calculated snub – a rejection of the request with contempt. Hence the exclamation *What?!* from Joanna. It would be tempting for you to ask students to continue this exchange, but rather foolhardy! If they can grasp the subtleties of the above explanation, you should rest content.

8a Linda does not want to be accused of being greedy – although she is!

b She clearly does not know Mrs Tidmarsh very well or she would not have to use such an indirect request.

c It would seem that Mrs Tidmarsh is somewhat older than Linda; note her use of the familiar *dear*, even though Linda calls her <u>Mrs</u> Tidmarsh.

Play the model exchanges on the cassette for students to listen to, repeat and practise. Monitor for intonation, etc.

Exercise 1

Supplementary exercise   Get students to provide written continuations of each phrase and then practise saying them aloud. Monitor for tone, appropriateness and effect.

Exercises 2a and 2b

Suggested answers are as in the tapescript for Exercise 3. Any deviant responses should be examined for differences in tone, appropriateness and effect.

Exercise 3

Remember to pause the cassette recorder to give students time to respond.

Tapescript (a)

1 You want your teacher to give you an example before you do your work. You say . . . (*Pause*)

sʀ Would you mind giving me an example before I do the exercise?
2 You want your neighbour to look after your cat while you're away on holiday. You say . . . (*Pause*)
sʀ I was wondering if you could possibly look after Tiddles while I'm away?
3 You want the man opposite you on the train to close the window – it's freezing! You say . . . (*Pause*)
sʀ Would you mind closing the window?
4 You want the woman opposite you on the train to let you close the window – it's freezing! You say . . . (*Pause*)
sʀ Would you mind if I closed the window?
5 You want your boss to meet you after work to discuss your problem. He's very busy now. You say . . . (*Pause*)
sʀ I know it's not a good time to talk now, but would it be possible to meet after work and talk about my problem?
6 You want the young people in the next house to stop playing their music so loudly. You say . . . (*Pause*)
sʀ Would you be so kind as to turn that music down?

Notes on the tapescript

1 A fairly direct request is needed. *Would you mind giving . . . ?* is the most appropriate of the six given.
2 A more difficult task requires a more indirect request form. Check the pitch range against the model on cassette. High-head, fall + rise nucleus on Tiddles and *away*.
3 and 4 Contrast *Would you mind . . . -ing?* with *Would you mind if I . . . ?* Check students' understanding of the distinction between the two forms in similar situations.
5 Making a request to someone senior calls for formal elaboration – the indirect *Would it be possible to . . . ?*
6 Irritation gives rise to the over-polite form. Check for even stress throughout. Upper part of the voice range. High-head with high-fall nucleus on *music*.

Tapescript (b)

7 Do you mind if I share your office for the day – mine's being redecorated? (*Pause*)
sʀ No, of course not, go ahead.
8 Do you think we could change the day for the committee meeting from Tuesdays to Thursdays? (*Pause*)
sʀ I'm afraid that's not possible. I'm not available on Thursdays.
9 I was wondering if you could possibly write an article for our new local magazine? (*Pause*)
sʀ I'd very much like to help you, but I'm afraid I just haven't got the time at the moment.
10 Ah, there you are! I was wondering if I could possibly borrow your golf-clubs this weekend. I'm afraid I've broken half of mine! (*Pause*)

sᴿ I'd rather not, actually. I never lend them to anyone.
11 Oh, er, I wonder if you could show these visitors round the building?
(*Pause*)
sᴿ Yes, of course. I'd be delighted to.
12 Would you go and see Mr Parkhurst as soon as you've got a moment? He
says it's quite important. (*Pause*)
sᴿ Oh, all right. If I really have to.

Notes on the tapescript

7 This revises student comprehension of the correct affirmative
response to the *Do you mind if . . . ?* construction. It's the only
possible answer of the six provided.
8 This is a formal refusal in a public context.
9 This indirect request, which is also complimentary, provokes a
gentle rejection consisting of an apologetic explanation. Student
tone should reflect regret, with nucleus on *time*.
10 The request does not instil confidence, thus the firm refusal.
Actually is used to soften the impact slightly.
11 The nucleus is on *deli̲ghted*.
12 This is reluctant acceptance. Nucleus fall-rise on *have*. Low pitch
range is needed in contrast to high pitch for No. 11. See the
cassette sᴿs.

Exercise 4

Tapescript

1 You want the accounts manager of your company to send you all the sales
figures for last year. You've just got him on the telephone. You say . . .
(*Pause*)
sᴿ Would you mind sending me over all the sales figures for last year?
2 You're asking a sales assistant in a furniture store if you could have a table
you like in wood, not brass. You say . . . (*Pause*)
sᴿ Would it be possible to have this table in wood, not brass?
3 You want a fellow student to lend you his notes, but it's just before the
exams and you think he may need them himself. (*Pause*)
sᴿ I know it's not a good time, but do you think I could possibly borrow
your notes?
4 You're getting rather annoyed with a man who is smoking his pipe in a
small airless restaurant. You ask him to stop while people are trying to eat.
(*Pause*)
sᴿ Would you be so kind as to stop smoking your pipe while people are
trying to eat?
5 You've already asked your friend's mother if she will let you borrow her
lawn-mower for a few days, and she hasn't been very co-operative. But you
really need that lawn-mower, so you say . . . (*Pause*)
sᴿ If I could borrow it – just for a few days – I'd be very grateful.
6 And another question like the last one. You want to impress a new friend by

borrowing your uncle's very expensive limousine to take her to dinner. Your uncle's hesitating about letting you use it. You say . . . (*Pause*)
sr I know it's very valuable, but if you could let me use it – just for tonight – I really would be grateful.
Now here are six more direct requests. Answer them as naturally as you can.
7 a   Would it be possible to talk about your plans for next year some time on Tuesday?
    Accept. (*Pause*)
    sr Yes, of course.
8 Do you think we could use the school's tennis court for our annual championship?
    Agree to this, officially. (*Pause*)
    sr I see no objection to that.
9 I'd like to change this red sports car for that black hatchback.
    It's not possible – your company never changes cars. (*Pause*)
    sr I'm afraid that's not possible. We never change cars.
10 Would you mind if I stayed at your house when I visit your country?
    It's a pity, but you just haven't got room. (*Pause*)
    sr I'm awfully sorry, but you see we just haven't got enough room.
11 Excuse me, would you be so kind as to close the window?
    Agree – reluctantly. (*Pause*)
    sr Oh, all right . . . if you insist.
12 I was wondering if I could possibly take some of your records for a few days – I'd like to record them.
    Reject this request politely – you never lend records in case they're damaged. (*Pause*)
    sr Well I'd rather not, actually. I never lend my records to anyone – they get damaged so easily, don't they?!

Notes on the tapescript

1 This is a business situation. The sr is a standard unemotional request. There is no need for over-elaboration.
2 This is a slightly more formal sr, but again no indirectness is implied.
3 The situation calls for an indirect approach. The sr provides an acknowledgement of bad timing and an indirect request.
4 sr revises cold politeness containing irritation, but many variants are possible. Do not correct more indirect forms.
5 This revises the support function of the phrase *If . . . I'd be grateful.* Revise other methods of secondary requesting, if necessary.
6 As for 5.
    At the end of the whole exercise, use the six situations above as the basis for student roleplay in pairs, continuing the conversations started above.
7 Straight acceptance is all that is required here.

8 sᴿ revises impersonal acceptance.

9 This is an official rejection prefaced by a formal apology.

10 A more personal tone is required here, with a stronger apology and *just* for emphasis.

11 An annoyed request provokes a grudging acceptance, but do not correct more polite acceptances unless they are totally at odds with the request.

12 Contrast the sᴿ here with the sᴿ in Exercise 3, No. 10. A fuller and more effusive refusal and explanation is required.

Exercise 5

Ask students to suggest variants on the phrases reviewed. Allow them to add acceptable variants to their books, unless they appear in Unit 7 of Section A or Section C.

Pairwork, groupwork and roleplay suggestions

Refer back to the students' written continuations of the phrases in Exercise 1 (supplementary exercise). In the light of subsequent practice (Exercises 2, 3, 4, 5), ask them to use these monitored sentences as the basis for conversation in pairs or groups, extending or developing their original ideas.

Unit 8 **Inviting, suggesting, accepting and refusing**

Checkpoint

Notes for guidance

1a Frank must be a manager of some kind – finance or marketing. Linda must be his secretary.
 b He is trying out his thoughts on Linda, but as he will know her quite well, he might expect her to make a suggestion. She can't be sure if he wants a suggestion or not.
 c Richard wouldn't have been expecting it at all.

2a Simon has gone to see Brian to borrow money.
 b He has had a sudden demand for tax.
 c No, he has come to borrow money.
 d Simon probably thought that it wasn't worth employing an accountant.
 e He thought an accountant's fees would be so high that it would cost him more than he would save.

3a Betty probably doesn't know Brian Carter personally. She calls him by his surname, and refers to herself as Betty Hamilton.
 b Richard probably knows him reasonably well – probably on a business footing.
 c Yes, they have.
 d It is normal when talking to someone you don't know to preface an invitation in this way. The use of past tense forms is common, as it gives the other person the opportunity to decline without feeling they are upsetting your plans.
 e The time is fixed. The use of the past perfect form has the same function as described in the previous note.
 f He probably would like to come.
 g He hasn't refused, though he probably needs to check and then ring back to confirm he can come.
Roleplay Students to create Brian's half of the conversation and then act out the dialogue in pairs.

Play the model exchanges on the cassette for the students to listen to, repeat and practise. Monitor for intonation, etc.

Exercise 1

Notes

That's very kind of you indeed. High-fall nucleus on *indeed.*
I would be delighted to come. High-fall nucleus on *delighted.*

I would love to come, but . . . High-fall nucleus on *love*.
Supplementary exercise   Get students to provide written continuations
of each phrase and then practise saying them aloud. Monitor for tone,
appropriateness and effect.

Exercise 2

Suggested answers are as in the tapescript for Exercise 3. Any deviant
responses should be examined for differences in tone, appropriateness
and effect.

Exercise 3

Remember to pause the cassette recorder to give students time to
respond.

Tapescript

1 We've just had a very stiff letter from the bank manager about our overdraft.
  (*Pause*)
  SR In the circumstances, I think you should go and see him.
2 We're having a cocktail party for our regular customers on Friday evening,
  and wondered if you'd like to join us? (*Pause*)
  SR That's extremely kind of you. We would be delighted to come. Thank
  you very much indeed.
3 We seem to be having a bit of trouble with our photocopier at the moment.
  (*Pause*)
  SR Can I suggest that you get in touch with the manufacturer?
4 Some strange man has been hanging round the office. It's a bit worrying.
  (*Pause*)
  SR The best thing would be to contact the police.
5 We've just had another demand from the Inspector of Taxes. That can't be
  right. (*Pause*)
  SR Wouldn't it be a good idea if we sent it on to the accountants?
6 I've been told that it would be more economical as well as more efficient to
  computerize our office. (*Pause*)
  SR I would certainly recommend that you should look into it carefully.
7 Would you believe it! Wyatt and Co. have just sent us another order when
  they haven't even paid for the last one yet! (*Pause*)
  SR The best thing would be to tell them that they can't have any more credit,
  don't you think?
8 I was thinking of having a little party on Saturday, and wondered if you'd
  like to come? (*Pause*)
  SR That's very kind of you indeed. I'd love to come, but I'm afraid I'm going
  to be away then. Thank you very much all the same.

Notes on the tapescript

1 An alternative suggestion is *The best thing would be to . . . don't you
  think?*

2 The refusal form would be equally appropriate. We have chosen to accept.

3 The first speaker is merely making a comment, not implying that she would like a suggestion at all, so this tentative approach would perhaps be most suitable.

4 This is a worrying situation; a suggestion is clearly in order, so we use a much more direct form.

5 Syntactic considerations make this the only available option.

6 The first speaker's statement would encourage a recommendation rather than a suggestion.

7 Another suitable suggestion form would be: *In the circumstances, I think you should* . . . See note 1.

8 We have chosen to refuse. An acceptance would be equally appropriate.

Exercise 4

Tapescript

1 One of my suppliers has just refused to give me any more credit until I have cleared my account with them. (*Pause*)
sr In the circumstances, I think you should pay them what you owe them.

2 Mr Hamilton, it seems we haven't got enough stock of model B7 to fill Jackman and Co.'s order . . . and they are our best customers. (*Pause*)
sr In the circumstances, I think we should offer them a better model at a special discount.

3 Er . . . I think we ought to invite Mr Rogers of the *Daily Echo* to our reception for the press next Friday evening. Would you ring him up and ask him, please? (*Pause*)
sr Mr Rogers, we are having a reception for the press next Friday evening and wondered if you'd like to come.

4 Imagine you are Simon Rogers and respond to the invitation. Listen again.
   Mr Rogers, we are having a reception for the press next Friday evening and wondered if you'd like to come. (*Pause*)
sr That's very kind of you and I would love to come, but I'm afraid I'm busy that evening. Thank you very much all the same.

5 Wyatt and Co. have let us down over our last order. That's the fourth time they've done it this year. (*Pause*)
sr The best thing would be to cancel the order and give our business to someone else, don't you think?

6 I've got to fly to New York next week. I can never decide what airline to go on. (*Pause*)
sr I would certainly recommend that you should fly British Airways. They really do look after you well.

7 I don't see that there is much point in discussing this any further until the end-of-year figures have been released. (*Pause*)
sr Can I suggest then that we should adjourn this discussion until we have the figures?

8 I'm not sure that I have fully understood the significance of this unit. (*Pause*)
  sʀ Can I suggest that you should go back and review the whole unit, then?

Notes on the tapescript

1 See note to Exercise 3, nos. 1 and 7.
2 In this case the form of suggestion given seems clearly the most appropriate, as there is no real alternative course of action if they are to remain best customers.
3 There is no need to be especially polite; this is an official function.
4 Other forms of acceptance would be equally suitable.
5 See note 1 above.
6 The prompt looks for a recommendation rather than a suggestion.
7 The prompt is a rather final statement, so the suggestion needs to be tentative.
8 Again, a tentative suggestion is called for so as not to give offence.

Exercise 5

Refer back to the students' written continuations of the phrases in
Exercise 1 (supplementary exercise). In the light of subsequent practice
(Exercises 2, 3, 4, 5), ask them to use these monitored sentences as the
basis for conversation in pairs or groups, extending or developing
their original ideas.

Unit 9 **Approving and disapproving**

Checkpoint

Notes for guidance

1a Nigel's phrase, *(it) leaves a lot to be desired*, signifies strong disapproval: he doesn't like the scheme at all.

  b His first sentence makes it clear that he is not against <u>all</u> proposals in this area – just this particular one. This is another example of 'limiting' language: Nigel appears to be a thinking, reasonable man with a balanced viewpoint, and so he is more likely to be believed and his opinions respected.

2a Almost! Mrs Allison does leave an exit door for herself by the use of *look* and *seem* instead of *are*.

  b It would appear that Mrs Allison is either a school inspector, or a retired teacher/headmistress on a return visit, or perhaps one of the school governors. At any rate her confidence proclaims that she feels superior to Louise, who could therefore be her successor as head teacher or a junior teacher.

  c They are probably in a school.

  d Mrs Allison's hesitation and use of *just one thing, however . . .* indicate that she has found <u>something</u> to criticise.

Roleplay Ask students to continue this exchange in the characters of Mrs Allison and Louise (or their male equivalents).

3a They are discussing a computer for use in the company.

  b The directness of Derek's questions shows that he is the boss. Leigh is probably Derek's general or finance manager.

  c Leigh is content, not more, with the machine's capacity in the given areas, but he minimises his content in order to make his reservations more telling – reservations which he has to make tactfully in view of the family connections.

  d His second sentence really means: *Even though it's your brother's company, the computer is much too expensive.*

  e He employs this indirect form for the reason given in (c), and because of his subordinate position to Derek.

Roleplay Ask students to imagine similar areas where they must show tactful disapproval in a subordinate situation. The roleplay should be done in pairs. Monitor and discuss.

4a Mr Packham is showing Alice round a flat or bed-sitting room.

  b Alice is an ordinary person.

  c Not very formal.

  d Packham is using friendly, familiar language in an attempt to convince Alice of the room's suitability.

e The formality of her language (in contrast to Mr Packham's familiarity) is caused by her irritation at being misled about the room.

Roleplay Ask students to continue this exchange as the same characters, then as themselves in the role of prospective tenant and landlord/landlady.

5a Not at all.

b Dr Wallis is expressing regret for having to disapprove; disappointment rather than anger at Sutton's school performance.

c His tag question invites Sutton to agree with his disapproval as a first step towards changing the boy's behaviour.

d Sutton's apology is standard British schoolboy shorthand when criticised or rebuked. It does not necessarily imply that he intends to reform! Discuss this teacher–pupil relationship with the class. Is it universal behaviour?

6a Both Henry and David are disappointed in the object and disapprove of it. David is trying to make the best of a bad job, and to find a redeeming positive feature – but without much success.

b The rewriting exercise is designed to illustrate how difficult it is to re-phrase even such a simple exchange without either losing subtlety of communication or lengthening each utterance disproportionately.

Play the model exchanges on the cassette for students to listen to, repeat and practise. Monitor for intonation, etc.

Exercise 1

The phrases are listed in descending order of approval down to *There's something to be said for it . . .*, then descending through reserved disapproval to full disapproval.

Supplementary exercise Get students to provide written continuations of each phrase and then practise saying each one aloud. Monitor for tone, appropriateness and effect.

Exercise 2

Suggested answers are as in the tapescript for Exercise 3. Any deviant responses should be examined for differences in tone, appropriateness and effect.

Exercise 3

Tapescript

1 Ah, there you are. Good. Look, I was wondering . . . about next year's salary levels . . . The thing is . . . How do you feel about accepting a 5 per cent cut in salary next year . . . for the good of the company, of course . . . ? (*Pause*)
SR I'm afraid that's simply not acceptable. If anything, I would be asking for a 5 per cent rise next year. After all, the company's doing very well, and I don't . . .

2 So, ladies and gentlemen, the school would like to know whether the week's trip to France for form LT5 meets with your approval or not. Er yes . . . er . . . what is your reaction? (*Pause*)
SR I'm very much in favour of it. It will be very good for the children's general education.

3 Here it is then, a beautiful piece – and, as you know, we've been trying to find something like this for you for three months now. There! What do you think? Only £890! (*Pause*)
SR Er . . . I'm afraid it's not really what I had in mind at all. I'm actually looking for something less ornate – and less expensive.

4 (*On the telephone.*) Hello! Great news! I've won our local marathon race! (*Pause*)
SR Well done! I didn't know you went in for that sort of thing!

5 How are you finding the new Bimbo? Good on the road, is it? (*Pause*)
SR I really am very impressed with it. It's certainly a great improvement on the last model. A very wise choice, if I may say so!

6 Oh, there's the hi-fi you got from the mail-order firm. Jolly good company, they are. What's the hi-fi like, then? (*Pause*)
SR Well, I'm afraid it's not quite what I expected. It doesn't look as good as it did in the catalogue – and the sound leaves a lot to be desired, too!

7 There, what do you think? I've put all the A to M's in the blue files and all the N to Zs in the greens! Is that all right? (*Pause*)
SR Hmm . . . It seems to be perfectly satisfactory. I don't think there was much wrong with the old system, though!

Notes on the tapescript

1 Strong disapproval is called for in a public situation. The suggested response provides a counter-argument and rationale. Monitor students' responses for the same. Note that the heavy stress falls on *simply*.

2 Public approval is sought and provided in SR.

3 Disapproval is conveyed with delicacy, as the seller has gone to some trouble. Point out the use of *really* as a modifier, not an intensifier. Discuss this together with the use of *actually* in the next sentence. Revise if necessary.

4 Enthusiastic approval is demanded in this situation. Note the intonation pattern on the exclamation of surprise, *Well done!* – high-head + high-fall nucleus. In the following sentence there is rising-head, high-fall on *in*, with low tail.

5 The employee's subordinate situation calls for a public expression of warm approval. The sr provides formal enthusiasm: *I am very impressed*, followed by a continuation that flatters the judgement of the first speaker. In the second sentence there is a low pre-head, high-head on *great*; high-fall nucleus on *last*.

6 The first speaker needs to be let down lightly. sr begins by expressing disappointment, and then gathers in strength and interest. Ask students to continue this exchange at the end of the whole exercise.

7 Grudging approval is called for. Point out the change of intent if *seems* or *satisfactory* are more heavily stressed. If *seems*, the speaker is not sure it is satisfactory; if *satisfactory*, he is sure but doesn't like it! The continuation provided makes it clear that the second option has been chosen.

Exercise 4

Pause the tape on the beep cues, but give students time to think before they respond.

Tapescript

1 You're at a conference and are asked if you approve of using video to teach English. You think it's great! (*Beep*)
sr I'm very much in favour of it. It's new, it's exciting, and it's highly motivating.

2 You're just leaving a meeting with your lawyer. You're pleased with the work he's done for you, but think his last bill was rather high! (*Beep*)
sr I don't like to mention this, but I did think your last bill was a bit high.

3 You're in charge of a department in a large store. One of the assistants is always late and unhelpful to customers. Your boss asks what you think of his conduct. (*Beep*)
sr I'm afraid it leaves a great deal to be desired.

4 You are announcing the results of a competition to find the best photographer in the school. The winner, Marion Wilson, is popular with everyone. (*Beep*)
sr I'm pleased to be able to say that the winner of this year's best photographer competition is Marion Wilson and I'm sure everyone will join with me in congratulating her on a well-deserved triumph.

5 The boat you and your friends have hired for your holiday is very bad. You are trying to cheer them up, and the boat does have one good feature – it has enough space for everyone to sleep comfortably. You say . . . (*Beep*)
sr Well, there's something to be said for it, I suppose. I mean, it's big enough for all of us, isn't it?

6 Your colleague always asks you for your approval of his written work. Up to

now you've been polite, although it's not very good, but you finally need to express your disapproval of his latest report. You say . . . (*Beep*)
sr Look, I'm sorry to have to say this, but it's really not very good, you know.
7 Although you generally approve of the work the plumber has done for you, the central heating system is making a rather strange noise. You say . . . (*Beep*)
sr There is just one thing, Mr Burgin. The central heating system seems to be making rather a strange noise.
8 Your teacher asks you if you like using *Speaking Skills*. You know that your command of English has improved dramatically since you started studying it. You say . . . (*Beep*)
sr I really am very impressed with it, sir.
9 The same teacher asks if you think it's a good idea for everyone in the school to spend a few days in England to put *Speaking Skills* into practical use. You think this is a splendid idea. (*Beep*)
sr I'm very much in favour of this idea. It would give us all the practice we need.
10 You asked the car salesman to show you a good but inexpensive sports car. Instead he shows you a Ferrari! You say . . . (*Beep*)
sr That's not really what I had in mind at all – it's far too expensive for me.

Notes on the tapescript

1 A conference requires a public register. sr provides firm approval plus supportive explanation.
2 Tactful disapproval is introduced by an apologetic phrase.
3 This is an official expression of disapproval. Monitor for similiar register in students' variants.
4 This practises an introductory phrase to elicit public approval. Revise the second structure in the sentence at the end of the whole exercise.
5 Few if any variants are possible in this 'cheering-up' situation. Check for 'half-convinced' tone: fall + rise on *big* and *it*.
6 Irritation is called for in language and tone. Point out the use of *Look* as an introduction to similar expressions of discontent. The second phrase, *I'm sorry to have to say this*, softens the impact slightly. But, nonetheless, strong disapproval is necessary, thus *it's* . . . *not very good* + tag, *you know*.
7 sr expresses disapproval or discontent with a particular problem. Nucleus on *one* in the first sentence.
8 An enthusiastic tone is essential here! sr: emphatic stepping head, high-fall nucleus on *impressed*.
9 As in No. 8, a formal teacher–student relationship is assumed. Hence the formal nature of both approving phrases in the sr.
10 sr revises a disapproving phrase from earlier in the unit. Extend and practise its use in various shopping or choosing situations.

Exercise 5

Ask students to suggest variants on the phrases reviewed. Allow them to add acceptable variants to their books, unless they appear in Unit 9 of Section A or Section C.

Pairwork, groupwork and roleplay suggestions

Refer back to the students' written continuations of the phrases in Exercise 1 (supplementary exercise). In the light of subsequent practice (Exercises 2, 3, 4, 5), ask them to use these monitored sentences as the basis for conversation in pairs or groups, extending or developing their original ideas.

Unit 10 **Apologising**

Checkpoint

Notes for guidance

1a Justin is quite late; he says he was *rather held up*.
  b Joanna accepts his apology neutrally.
  c A more profuse apology by Justin would require more elaborated acceptance forms, and this in itself would disrupt the meeting even more than his late arrival. Such apologies should be made to the chairman in person after the meeting.

2a Most definitely. Henry is in danger of losing the business.
  b Perhaps Henry could be a bit more profuse in his first apology. *I can't apologise enough* might have been a bit better.
  c It is standard politeness to modify an aggressive statement with a phrase like, *I'm sorry to say* when talking to business contacts or members of the public.
  d Shirley knows that Henry didn't advise them. *It seems* is a standard phrase when making complaints and is used to soften the blow.
  e Henry's second apology is sincere, though a bit lame.
  f Shirley says, *I'm sorry to have to tell you* . . . because one always apologises before giving bad news.

3a See note 2f above.
  b Frank knows how the repayment periods compare.
  c Frank is using a standard phrase. See 2d above.
  d Not really; it is an exit line to close the discussion.

Play the model exchanges on the cassette for the students to listen to, repeat and practise. Monitor for intonation, etc.

Exercise 1

I do apologise. High-fall nucleus on *do.*
I really must (have to) apologise. High-fall nucleus on *must (have).*
I can't apologise enough. High-fall nucleus on *enough.*
Otherwise there are no particular intonational problems to highlight.
Supplementary exercise Get students to provide written continuations of each phrase and then practise saying them aloud. Monitor for tone, appropriateness and effect.

Exercise 2

Suggested answers are as in the tapescript for Exercise 3. Any deviant responses should be examined for differences in tone, appropriateness and effect.

Exercise 3

Students should pause their cassette recorders to give themselves time to respond.

Tapescript

1 Hello, this is Kenneth Brown speaking. Could I speak to Mr Carter immediately on a matter of some urgency, please? (*Pause*)
  sr I hope you'll excuse me for interrupting you, but the chairman would like to speak to you urgently.
2 I've come to find out whether I've been accepted for the job. (*Pause*)
  sr I'm sorry, but I'm afraid I have to tell you that we are unable to accept your application.
3 Good morning, I'm ringing to find out what has happened to that quotation you were going to send me. (*Pause*)
  sr I do apologise for not sending it to you last week, but I'm afraid I was sent away in an emergency.
4 Hello, I understand it's about this week's consignment. (*Pause*)
  sr I'm sorry to have to tell you that I'm afraid we won't be able to despatch your consignment until next Monday.
5 Well, what happened to you at the meeting yesterday? (*Pause*)
  sr I can't apologise enough for missing it. I'm afraid I forgot to check my diary.
6 Ah, finally . . . you've brought our typewriter back. (*Pause*)
  sr I must apologise for not bringing it before now, but I'm afraid it wasn't ready.
7 Oh, hello. What about it? Can we meet when I suggested? (*Pause*)
  sr I'm sorry to say I will be away. Perhaps we could meet next week.
8 Are you sure you can't stay and have lunch with us? (*Pause*)
  sr I hope you'll excuse me for not staying. I'm afraid I have to get back for a board meeting.

Notes on the tapescript

In this exercise the form of the apology is automatically determined by the lexical or syntactical selection in the response.
1 A formal interruption phrase is required.
2 This is an apology before giving bad news.
3 A broken promise requires a fairly firm apology.
4 This is an apology for bad news.
5 A very sincere apology is needed in this situation.
6 A promise was broken, so a fairly firm apology is required.
7 The news is slightly unwelcome, but the apology shouldn't be overdone.
8 Only a very general apology is needed.

Exercise 4

Tapescript

1 You arrived late at a meeting because you were caught up in a traffic jam, and came in while they were in the middle of discussing an important item. The meeting is now over. Go and apologise sincerely to the chairman. (*Pause*)
    SR I really must apologise for arriving late at the meeting. I'm afraid I was caught up in a traffic jam.
2 You promised to meet someone tomorrow to discuss a new project. Unfortunately you have had to change all your plans. Tell him or her. (*Pause*)
    SR I'm sorry to say that I'm afraid I won't be able to meet you tomorrow. I have had to change all my plans.
3 Someone has come to your bank to borrow some money. Unfortunately you cannot accept this client's application. Tell her so. (*Pause*)
    SR I regret to say that I'm afraid we cannot accept your application.
4 You have been lent a typewriter by the business next door. You have kept it rather a long time. Apologise as you give it back. (*Pause*)
    SR I do apologise for keeping your typewriter for such a long time.
5 You had promised to do some work for someone. Unfortunately you have forgotten all about it. He is on the phone wanting to know why it hasn't been done yet. Apologise and admit what has happened. (*Pause*)
    SR I can't apologise enough for not having done it yet. I'm afraid I had forgotten all about it.
6 You have been asked if your company would illustrate a book. You are not interested, as it is not really your line of business. You are an industrial design firm. Tell them so. (*Pause*)
    SR I'm sorry to have to tell you that I'm afraid we can't do it. It's not in our line of business.
7 Someone arrived to see you twenty minutes ago, but you haven't seen her yet. You have had the chairman of the company on the phone. Apologise for keeping her waiting for so long. (*Pause*)
    SR I hope you'll excuse me for keeping you waiting so long. I've had the company chairman on the phone.
8 You have been trying to get hold of someone on the telephone since yesterday afternoon, when you promised to let him have some information, but you haven't been able to contact him up to now. Apologise for not letting him have the information before. (*Pause*)
    SR I do apologise for not letting you have the information before, but I haven't been able to get hold of you.

Notes on the tapescript

1 A sincere apology is required by the prompt. Any of the firmer apologies in the model phrase list will do.
2 Apologise first before giving bad news.
3 Giving bad news in a serious situation. This is a slight variation on the phrase in the list of models.

4 You've kept the typewriter rather a long time, so a fairly firm apology is required.
5 A promise has been broken, so a sincere apology is required.
6 The news is bad, but no blame can attach to you, so it isn't too serious.
7 A general apology is required – your visitor will know that you can't hang up on the company chairman.
8 Only a moderately firm apology is required, since it is not really your fault.

Exercise 5

Ask students to suggest variants on the phrases reviewed. Allow them to add acceptable variants to their books, unless they appear in Unit 10 of Section A or Section C.

Pairwork, groupwork and roleplay suggestions

Apologies can be practised in any situation requiring complaints, for example complaints to shops for faulty goods, poor workmanship, etc. For complaints see Unit 9, Section C.

Refer back to the students' written continuations of the phrases in Exercise 1 (supplementary exercise). In the light of subsequent practice (Exercises 2, 3, 4, 5), ask them to use these monitored sentences as the basis for conversation in pairs or groups, extending or developing their original ideas.

Section C
Further developments, colloquial English and related functions

Unit 1 **Giving yourself time**

As in Unit 1, Section A, and Unit 1, Section B, there is a slightly different format for this unit.

Checkpoint

Notes for guidance

1a Joanna and Simon are certainly friends – probably reasonably close friends.

 b We don't think the difference between British and American English is easy to explain.

 c Joanna and Simon are both trying to agree on a definition and need to refine it with each alternative.

 d *Forthright, straight from the shoulder,* and *direct* mean almost exactly the same thing.

2a Linda and Beatrice are quite good friends.

 b Linda needs to cast her mind back to think what it was she and Michael had.

 c 'Kow dom' is completely different from English food and so is difficult to describe accurately. She needs to try to find the right word.

 d The comparison between 'kow dom' and porridge is a difficult one, and Linda needs to show that she doesn't mean it to be taken literally, though it is the best she can do.

3a The first part of the statement up to and including the insertion of Brian's (Mr Carter's) name is used by Henry to give himself time. So is the qualification of the programme of development (*we have been reviewing*), and the use of *How shall I put it?* The rather ponderous formal way of speaking also lends weight to what is a rather thin statement.

 b Henry's project is not doing very well and he needs to find a way of putting it which, while not actually a lie, doesn't sound too negative. Brian Carter doesn't want to waste time searching for a more exact rephrasing of Henry's estimate.

 c Henry uses eight phrases to give himself time: *Oh well*; the repetition of Brian Carter's name; *I think you will agree that . . .*; unnecessary repetition of *on your investment*; *er; while not up to what we had originally predicted . . .*; *er; perhaps we can say . . .* He needs time to try and counteract the negative bias of Brian Carter's comment.

Model exchanges

Play the model exchanges on the cassette for students to listen to, repeat and practise. Monitor for intonation, etc.

Exercise 1

Intonation note   The phrases introduced here are all uttered on a mid-level tone.
Supplementary exercise   Get students to provide written continuations of each phrase and then practise saying them aloud. Monitor for tone, appropriateness and effect.

Exercises 2, 3 and 4

Remember to pause the cassette recorder to give students time to respond. The selection of hesitation techniques in these exercises cannot be controlled. Those given here and on the tape are merely those that a native speaker used when confronted with these questions.

Tapescript for Exercise 2

1 Which do you think are the three most important of the points given? (*Pause*)
   SUGGESTED RESPONSE Oh . . . that's a difficult question . . . mmm . . . first . . . er . . . corrosion protection . . . um . . . secondly . . . let me see . . . er . . . fuel economy . . . and thirdly . . . um . . . shall we say . . . safety bodywork design.
2 Which do you think are the three least important? (*Pause*)
   SR Ah . . . well . . . firstly eye-catching appearance, secondly . . . um . . . first-class performance . . . and finally . . . um . . . it's difficult . . . um . . . ruggedness.
3 Which do you think is the most important feature overall? (*Pause*)
   SR Oh um . . . let me think . . . er . . . fuel economy.
4 Which do you think is the least important overall? (*Pause*)
   SR Oh, that's much easier . . . mm . . . eye-catching appearance.
5 Out of the six cars pictured, which do you think best combines the features in your order of preference? (*Pause*)
   SR Oh now, well . . . erm . . . I should say the Maestro does because . . . well . . . as well as my first three . . . er . . . it also has extremely good all-round visibility, and um . . . it's also comfortable . . . um . . . Yes, I'll take the Maestro.

Tapescript for Exercise 3

1 If you were invited out to dinner at one of these restaurants, which one would you prefer to go to, and why? (*Pause*)
   SR Oh ah . . . let me think . . . mm . . . it's difficult, isn't it . . . er . . . I think probably the Mayfair Restaurant . . . but why . . . mmm . . . because . . . well . . . I like steak and kidney pie.

2 You are in the Mayfair Restaurant. What would you like for each course? (*Pause*)

sr Right, now, let me see . . . um . . . What shall I have first? . . . Um . . . soup, I think, and then . . . er . . . oh yes, steak and kidney pie with boiled potatoes and vegetables, and to finish now . . . apple . . . no I've already had one pie . . . mm . . . it'll have to be ice-cream. OK?

3 What is chicken Maryland? (*Pause*)

sr Oh well, er, it's chicken pieces . . . cooked . . . I mean fried with, er, sort of fried corn things and well, er . . . I think fried bananas, isn't it?

4 What is shepherd's pie, served by the Piccadilly Restaurant? (*Pause*)

sr Yes, much better than chicken Maryland, I think . . . um . . . well, it's not really a pie, or, well, sort of . . . but it's made with mashed potato instead of pastry, and, er, kind of minced meat underneath. Delicious!

5 What would you have for each course at the Piccadilly Restaurant? (*Pause*)

sr Well, let me see . . . first course . . . erm . . . grapefruit cocktail's boring, so I'll have the egg mayonnaise . . . Hmm, let me think . . . it's . . . roast chicken, I think, with er . . . mm . . . creamed potatoes and . . . shall we say . . . beans . . . and to follow . . . er, fresh fruit salad, but without cream . . . and then coffee, too.

Tapescript for Exercise 4

1 You only have time to see three of the sights. Which three would you like to see most? (*Pause*)

sr Well, now, let me see . . . er . . . Houses of Parliament, then, erm . . . St Paul's Cathedral . . . and lastly . . . erm . . . Which one would I like to see? . . . Oh, Tower Bridge, I think.

2 Which one would you like to visit least of all? (*Pause*)

sr Which would I like to visit least of all? . . . That's a difficult question . . . erm . . . Nelson's Column or Speaker's Corner . . . Which? . . . Shall we say . . . Nelson's Column?

3 And which would you like to visit most of all? (*Pause*)

sr That's not easy either . . . erm . . . I think . . . oh dear . . . St Paul's Cathedral perhaps.

4 What three sights would you recommend a visitor to see in your own town or country?

Exercise 5

Refer back to the students' written continuations of the phrases in Exercise 1 (supplementary exercise). In the light of subsequent practice (Exercises 2, 3, 4, 5), ask them to use these monitored sentences as the basis for conversation in pairs or groups, extending or developing their original ideas.

Pairwork, groupwork and roleplay suggestions

As we stated in the notes to Unit 1, Section A, and Unit 1, Section B, the need for hesitation devices runs throughout the book and so we make no specific suggestions here.

Unit 2 **Encounters, greetings and goodbyes, introductions**

Checkpoint

Notes for guidance

1 The point of this exchange is to demonstrate a very common way of starting a conversation with a stranger.

  a Michael certainly feels more strongly about starting the conversation than about the problem of finding a seat.

  b Linda's repeated *Yes* shows that at first she offers minimal politeness.

  c However, her third speech shows greater warmth. Perhaps she finds Michael attractive?

  d It could be, *Do you make this journey every day?*

Roleplay   Students act out this situation in pairs, with similar conversations in cafés, parks, discos, etc. Monitor closely.

2a The first question demonstrates the difficulty of rephrasing such simple phrases as, *How's it going?* and *What've you been up to?* Use this as a basis for discussion with similar phrases, *How are you getting on?*, *How is it coming on?*, etc.

  b The second question draws attention to the <u>activity</u> implied in Shirley's enquiry – not appropriate when asking about relaxation.

  c They are clearly close friends or husband and wife.

3a, b Not really – in both cases. Both speakers show surprise, not necessarily warmth in their greetings. They could be close or distant acquaintances who have not met for some time. Justin's *What a nice surprise!* in particular could be simply a social formula: *nice* is a notoriously weak word.

4a *Shutting up* is here used to refer to a shop or place of business. It does not mean that Harry is going to stop talking.

  b Amanda could be either a secretary, shop assistant, or something similar. Check student comprehension of *I'll be off*, meaning *I am about to go*.

5a *Time gentlemen, please!* is the traditional cry of a pub landlord at closing time.

  b Presumably Henry has not noticed the time because he has been drinking.

6 Impossible to say. They are in a work situation, but their degree of familiarity is not apparent from this standard, relaxed but public form of address.

7 In contrast, Janet's farewell to Pierre is more personal and warmer in tone. She also makes use of expressions needed when saying goodbye for a longer period of time than in 6.

Play the model exchanges on the cassette for students to listen to, repeat and practise. Monitor for intonation, etc.

Exercise 1

Supplementary exercise   Get students to provide written continuations of each phrase and then practise saying them aloud. Monitor for tone, appropriateness and effect.

Exercise 2

Suggested answers are as in the tapescript for Exercise 3. Any deviant responses should be examined for differences in tone, appropriateness and effect.

Exercise 3

Remember to pause the cassette recorder to give students time to respond.

Tapescript

1 Lovely day, isn't it? (*Pause*)
   sr (a) Yes, beautiful, isn't it?
2 Over here on business, are you? (*Pause*)
   sr (b) Yes, I am, actually. How did you know?
3 (*Beep*)
   sr (c) Hello! What are you doing here?
   Ooooh! Fancy meeting you here!
4 (*Beep*)
   sr (a) How's it going?
   Oh, all right. What've you been up to?
5 (*Beep*)
   sr (b) It's getting late, I'm afraid.
   Oh, I'll be off then.
6 (*Beep*)
   sr (a) Bye! Have a good weekend!
   Bye! See you next week.
7 I'm off, then. See you. (*Pause*)
   sr (b) OK. Take care!
8 Thanks for everything. Take care of yourself, won't you? (*Pause*)
   sr (c) Yes, of course – and you too – you look after yourself!

Notes on the tapescript

1 sr assumes a willingness to continue the conversation. Note from

the intonation that it is not a genuine question. Option (b) is too dismissive, (c) surly.

2 SR is a polite continuation. (a) is aggressive, (c) brusque.

3 The response given is casual and idiomatic. (a) is far too formal to produce it, (b) is also too formal to produce it. Check nucleus on *you*, not *doing*.

4 The response given assumes a question about an activity – option (a) is therefore correct. (b) is a question on health. (c) is idiomatic for *What's the problem?* Discuss or revise.

5 The response given is a reaction to information conveyed, not a farewell in itself. Hence answer (b). (a) is the opposite, (c) is an inappropriate farewell. Nucleus high-fall on *off*.

6 The response given presumes a short-term (weekend) farewell, hence answer (a). (b) and (c) are both long-term farewells. Note rise-fall on monosyllable *Bye!*

7 The phrase given is casual and relaxed. Option (a) is too formal, (c) is acceptable, but in American not British usage. (b) is the correct option. Compare the use of *Take care* as an everyday goodbye, and *Take care of yourself* for longer-term farewells.

8 This follows from 7. The given phrase is a longer-term farewell. (a) accepts good wishes without reciprocating, and so is unacceptable. (b) doesn't make sense. (c) returns the warmth, and is therefore correct.

Exercise 4

Tapescript

1 You're at a conference on civil engineering. You suddenly see Mrs Thomas, the mother of your best friend, walking into the entrance hall. What do you say to her? (*Pause*)
SR Hello, Mrs Thomas. What are you doing here?

2 You're standing at the top of a big hill with a spectacular view of the surrounding countryside. There is one other person there with you – a stranger. You want to start a conversation with him – what do you say? (*Pause*)
SR Fantastic view, isn't it?

3 It's Friday night, and you've stayed late at the office to help finish some work. But now it's time to go. Your boss calls out, *It's 6.45.* You have a train to catch at 7.00! What do you say? (*Pause*)
SR Is it? I must dash! See you on Monday!

4 You're saying goodbye to some friends after work or school on a Friday night. You'll see them again on Monday. What do you say? (*Pause*)
SR Bye! Have a good weekend.

5 You've left your friend working on your car while you took a phone call indoors. Now you return. What do you say? (*Pause*)
SR Sorry about that. How's it going?

6 You've been standing in a bus queue in the pouring rain for more than ten minutes. One person has been waiting longer than you. Can you think of two phrases you could use to start a conversation? (*Pause*)
   sr Terrible weather, isn't it? *or*
   sr Been waiting long, have you?
7 You've just been chatting to a group of friends, but now it's time to go home. What do you say? (*Pause*)
   sr Well, I must be off – see you!
8 And now someone says to you, *Well, I must be off – see you!* What do you reply? (*Pause*)
   sr Yes, OK. Bye! Take care!

Notes on the tapescript

1 The situation calls for a surprised greeting of someone away from his or her expected environment.
2 Variants on *fantastic* are quite acceptable. But check for high-fall intonation pattern of the question-tag construction.
3 The situation calls for urgency and a farewell. Accept reasonable variants.
4 sr revises the standard Friday-night farewell. Accept variants, but revise the use of *Have a good weekend.*
5 The situation implies a question about the friend's progress while you have been away. Variants should express this. Do not allow a question that is too formal or too long.
6 Two srs are given, but other variants are possible. Use the srs to discuss the idiomatic shortenings given on tape, e.g. *Terrible weather . . .*, not *It is terrible weather . . .*; *Been waiting long . . .?* not, *Have you been waiting long . . .?* Practise further examples.
7 A statement of intention to leave, and a farewell, is all that is required here. Do not allow elaborate language forms.
8 As with 7, do not allow elaborate forms. The prompt is casual and relaxed.

Exercise 5

Ask students to suggest variants on the phrases reviewed. Allow them to add acceptable variants to their books, unless they appear in Unit 2 of Section A or Section B.

Pairwork, groupwork and roleplay suggestions

Refer back to the students' written continuations of the phrases in Exercise 1 (supplementary exercise). In the light of subsequent practice (Exercises 2, 3, 4, 5), ask them to use these monitored sentences as the basis for conversation in pairs or groups, extending or developing their original ideas.

Unit 3 **Information gathering**

Checkpoint

Notes for guidance

1a Janet and Simon are probably close friends.

 b Simon uses forms like these because he can't expect Janet to know the answers.

 c Janet is beginning to get annoyed; her use of *Look, why don't you . . .?* indicates that she doesn't want to be disturbed any more.

 d *Look* has a low-fall. *Why don't you phone the railway station?* uses the lower part of the voice range, and has a low-fall nucleus on railway.

2a Richard and Betty are probably married.

 b High-head. Fall+rise. Fall on *car*, rise on *Betty*.

 c Richard's question is a casual question, and should be put casually.

 d Betty is probably annoyed.

 e Her response is sarcastic in tone.

 f High-head. High-fall nucleus on *I*. Low-tail.

3a The question tags to Michael's questions should have high-fall intonation on the auxiliaries.

 b Michael is checking his information, as he says at the end. He merely wants confirmation.

 c The tag could have a low-rise on the auxiliary.

 d This would indicate that Michael had reason to suspect the contrary of the assertion.

 e Michael says *You do like . . .* because he needs to use emphatic stress on this assertion. In English, emphatic stress can only be carried by an auxiliary, not a main verb, so we use a positive form with the auxiliary.

Play the tape for the students to listen to, repeat and practice. Monitor for intonation, etc.

Exercise 1

Intonation notes

The first five question forms all require a fall+rise intonation pattern.

Supplementary exercise Get students to provide written continuations of each phrase and then practise saying each one aloud. Monitor for tone, appropriateness and effect.

Exercise 2

Suggested answers are as in the tapescript for Exercise 3. Any deviant responses should be examined for differences in tone, appropriateness and effect.

Exercise 3

Remember to pause the cassette recorder to give students time to respond.

Tapescript

1 You seem to be having a problem with that timetable. Can I help? (*Pause*)
   sr Do you by any chance know if there's a direct train to Littleton?
2 Have you lost something? What are you looking for? (*Pause*)
   sr Any idea where my book is?
3 Are you trying to find an address or something? (*Pause*)
   sr You wouldn't know where there's a good record shop, would you?
4 Well, I suppose we'd better go if we don't want to miss the start of the film.
   (*Pause*)
   sr You do want to come to the cinema, don't you?
5 What's that you're writing? A composition about London? (*Pause*)
   sr Have you any idea how many people live in London?
6 Do go ahead and smoke. I don't object. (*Pause*)
   sr You don't smoke, do you?
7 What's the matter? Have you lost your watch? (*Pause*)
   sr Any idea what the time is?
8 Why do you need the phone book? (*Pause*)
   sr You wouldn't know the dialling code for Paris, would you?

Notes on the tapescript

1 The sr doesn't expect an answer to the question.
2 A casual question is needed.
3 This is a slightly unusual question, so the past tense is used. A rising tag is required because you need to find out – you aren't checking.
4 You are checking. The friend doesn't seem sure, so a low-rise tag is needed.
5 You can't expect your friend to know the answer.
6 You are only checking. High-fall tag.
7 This is a casual question.
8 Again, people don't usually carry long-distance codes in their head. Low-rise tag.

Exercise 4

Tapescript

1 You are going on a sailing holiday with a friend. You're pretty sure he can swim, but you'd better just check. (*Pause*)
   sr You can swim, can't you?
2 You are on the way to a concert. Your friend is looking very worried and searching his pockets. You think he may have left the tickets behind. Check. (*Pause*)
   sr You haven't left the tickets behind, have you?
3 You have an appointment at the Connaught Hotel in London, but you don't know where it is. Your friend might know. Ask him. (*Pause*)
   sr Do you by any chance know where the Connaught Hotel is?
4 You are going to meet a friend at a concert, but she won't have much time to get there. You think she should be able to get there on time, but you aren't sure. (*Pause*)
   sr You should be able to get there on time, shouldn't you?
5 You have been to the theatre with a friend. She is looking very unhappy. Has the play upset her? You'd better check that she enjoyed it. (*Pause*)
   sr You did enjoy the play, didn't you?
6 Your friend is going away for some time. He has promised he will write, but perhaps you had better check that he won't forget. (*Pause*)
   sr You won't forget to write, will you?
7 You have just heard the expression 'Boxing Day', but you don't know why it is called that. Perhaps your friend has an idea. (*Pause*)
   sr Have you any idea why Boxing Day is called that?
8 You have been explaining something very complicated to your friend. You are pretty certain he understands, but perhaps you'd better check. (*Pause*)
   sr You do understand, don't you?

Notes on the tapescript

1 This is something you should be sure of, so use a high-fall tag.
2 Your friend seems worried. You only suspect the problem, so use low-rise tag. A high-fall tag would be sarcastic.
3 He might know, but you can't expect him to.
4 Since you aren't certain, use a low-rise tag.
5 Since she is apparently upset, don't be too assertive; use a low-rise tag.
6 The friend has promised to write, so you are merely checking. Use a high-fall tag.
7 This is a question he can't be expected to be able to answer.
8 You are only checking, so use a high-fall tag.

Exercise 5

Ask students to suggest variants on the phrases reviewed. Allow them to add acceptable variants to their books, unless they appear in Unit 3 of Section A or Section B.

Pairwork, groupwork and roleplay suggestions

Checking information:
1 Interview for a job. Use the checking technique to expand information on an application form.
2 Check preparations for a party, reception, or other formal occasions.

Unit 4 **Giving information and instructions**

Checkpoint

Notes for guidance

1a Shirley and Mr Conway are at the end of their conversation. The pattern of utterance and response in this exchange, *Fine, Marvellous* and *I'll look . . . then, I'll look forward to . . .* constitutes part of a system of pairs by which we signal the wish to close a conversation and the agreement to do so.

b Shirley and Mr Conway do not know each other at all. He has to describe himself so that Shirley will be able to recognise him.

c Mr Conway says, *Oh, by the way*, because he needs to re-open a conversation which has been nearly closed, in order to give information omitted earlier.

d He uses the order: physique, hair colour and style, eye colour, clothes.

e This is the order in which one's attention usually focuses on other people's appearance. Using this order makes the description easier for the listener to register the details and create a picture. See the notes on the model phrases.

2a Janet is being very friendly and sympathetic towards Henry, so presumably they know each other reasonably well.

b Henry and Janet are in the middle of this part of the conversation. The use of *Well* indicates a stage in a narrative, and *there I was* indicates that he has already mentioned being in the pub. See note on *Well* in the notes and phrases.

c Henry probably says *Well* with a high-fall in each case because he is picking up the story after an interruption or digression. If there is no interruption or digression it would be uttered with a low-fall.

d *Now* at the beginning of his second speech indicates that what follows is an elucidation of what has been said, rather than a new stage in the sequence of events.

e *Anyway* indicates a return to the main theme after a digression. *Roleplay* Exercise 3 in this unit is a development of this story. After doing Exercise 3, the whole story can be used for roleplay.

3 The use of a present perfect tense is a standard way of introducing a topic – particularly, as in this case, in a news report.

Play the model exchanges on the cassette for the students to listen to, repeat and practise. Monitor for intonation, etc.

Exercise 1

Intonation notes

Well: Either high- or low-fall. See note 2 above.
Now: Low-fall.
So: Long, drawn out fall-rise.
By the way: High-fall on *way*.
Incidentally: Usually a fall-rise to get back attention.
Anyway: High-fall on first syllable.

Exercise 2

Suggested answers are as in the tapescript for Exercise 3. Any deviant responses should be examined for differences in tone, appropriateness and effect.

Exercise 3

Remember to pause the cassette recorder to give students time to respond.

Tapescript

JANET How awful! . . . Poor you! . . . And did you find out what it was all about? (*Pause*)
HENRY Well, it seems that these three men had robbed a bank. They forced the cashier at gunpoint to hand over the money. Then they made their getaway in a van.
JANET Mmmm?
HENRY Well, after a while the van ran out of petrol and they had to abandon it . . .
JANET Yes?
HENRY Now, it was near the pub when they abandoned it. They saw my car and one of them came and found me.
JANET Yes, you said.
HENRY Well, I went to move my car and I was hit on the head as I told you . . . Anyway, they took my car keys and drove off in my car.
JANET Ah . . .
HENRY Now, someone had seen them and phoned the police. The police chased them and eventually caught them. They got my car and brought my car keys to the hospital.
JANET Oh, I see . . .
HENRY So that was it.

Notes on the tapescript

Since this unit is concerned with discourse, the exercise is not designed so that each sentence is interrupted by a reaction on tape. It is a continuation of the original dialogue. It would be best if students created the whole story from the pictures without any reference to the version on tape. The vocabulary is there in the book, because students should be concentrating on <u>how</u> they are telling the story, not on the words needed for the story.

Exercise 4

Tapescript

POLICEMAN Right, could you describe this individual you saw, please? As much as you can remember. (*Pause*)
WITNESS Well, he was very tall, about 6 foot 4 I think, with short wavy red hair. His eyes were brown . . . and . . . er . . . he had a scar over his right eye. Let me think . . . er . . . he was wearing a blue denim jacket and jeans . . . and . . . er . . . what else . . . er . . . oh, yes . . . a black sweater . . . and . . . er . . . that's all I can remember.
POLICEMAN Fine, thank you very much.

Notes on the tapescript

This exercise is treated as Exercise 3, but with a different discourse function. Again the exercise should concentrate on the ordering of the description, not on the vocabulary for describing an individual. Check how students' descriptions differ from the other witness's version.

Exercise 5

Exercise 5 in this unit is the free extension of Exercises 3 and 4. Again, students should pay more attention to discourse processes than to details of vocabulary.

Pairwork, groupwork and roleplay suggestions

The police officer interviewing a witness can clearly be developed for further practice. As a group practice, set up a game of murder with one student as a police officer interviewing the others as witnesses. Make sure that one of the witnesses is the murderer, and is lying in part and without a proper alibi. Open verdicts are unsatisfactory. You will need to use the units on getting information – A3, B3, C3.

For descriptions, students can compare where they are living, their homes or parents, former teachers, etc.

Unit 5 **Getting and giving opinions**

Checkpoint

Notes for guidance

1a After a concert performance of a Beethoven symphony.
  b The two speakers are friends.
  c This rephrasing exercise demonstrates the difficulty of rephrasing without (i) becoming too formal, or (ii) assuming <u>too</u> close a relationship.
  d Janet <u>was</u> sure the performance was good. The question tag is used only to reinforce her own opinion – it is a method of giving her opinion, in fact.
Roleplay Students should continue this situation, giving further opinions on the performance and related situations; e.g. after a pop concert, dinner at a restaurant, etc.

2a No. It is socially unacceptable to 'send food back' in a domestic situation.
  b Henry uses the tag to elicit confirmation of his belief.
  c Joanna uses the softener, *a bit*, to show that she is not over-concerned, <u>not</u> to show that she does not think the soup tastes funny.
  d Henry is not completely confident in sending the soup back – he asks for support with, *I don't know about you* . . . and softens it with, *I think* . . .
  e It seems unlikely that he is used to sending things back.
Roleplay Students to react to bad or unusual restaurant meals as the above characters; one of them less positive, the other more. Stop the situation before the waiter is called. (See Complaining, Unit 9, Section C).

3a This phrase is a very common colloquial means of checking understanding, and is over-used by a large part of the southern English population.
  b The mother's phrase serves a peace-keeping function, but clearly is to be taken seriously.
  c Her, *I don't know* . . . has the effect, and is meant to, of drawing the father into the conversation.
  d Father's tags do not weaken his argument; they are, if anything, colloquial intensifiers.
  e Father's question form is appropriate when requesting an unpleasant task – something you think the other person will not be very happy to do. Notice that this applies even between intimates.
Roleplay Students to develop this situation in groups as the above family.

4a Justin is also asking for his decision to be confirmed.
 b He is not sure he is going to go.
 c Sally's, *Do you know what I mean?* is another example of checking comprehension – also here used as a hesitation device.
 d Her, *Oh by the way* . . . changes the subject.
Roleplay   Students to develop this situation in pairs, with a third as the missing friend arriving and apologising, etc. (See Units A10, B10, C10).

5a Speakers employ a semi-elaborated code typically heard from TV/radio presenters. Here they are probably two TV football experts commentating on the second half of a match.
 b Phrases giving opinion:
   . . . it seems to me.
   Well, as I see it . . .
   Well, I may be wrong but I think . . .
   . . . if you ask me . . .
   . . . I still think . . .
 c Phrases asking for opinion:
   . . . you possibly know more about this than I do . . .
   Don't you agree?
   . . . what do you think about that?
   . . . (it) can't be a bad thing, can it?
   Do you see what I mean?
Note   Over the moon = very happy. *Sick as a parrot* = very unhappy.

Play the model exchanges on the cassette for students to listen to, repeat and practise. Monitor for intonation, etc.

Exercise 1

Supplementary exercise   Get students to provide written continuations of each phrase and then practise saying them aloud. Monitor for tone, appropriateness and effect.

Exercise 2

Suggested answers are as in the tapescript for Exercise 3. Any deviant responses should be examined for differences in tone, appropriateness and effect.

Exercise 3

Remember to pause the cassette recorder to give students time to respond.

Tapescript

1 Well, it's finished. (*Pause*)
  sr (a) Yes, lovely show, wasn't it?
2 Look at that man over there! (*Pause*)
  sr (b) Oh yes. He looks like Uncle Bill, doesn't he?
3 Oh, excuse me, you couldn't hold these books for me for a moment, could you? (*Pause*)
  sr (c) Yes, of course. Give them to me.
4 I saw Helge yesterday. (*Pause*)
  sr (a) Oh, that reminds me; her sister is coming to tea on Tuesday.
5 You probably know more about this than I do, but if you ask me, public transport is much better here than in London. (*Pause*)
  sr (c) Yes, I think you're probably right.
6 Well, I don't know about you, but I think they've improved the TV programmes a lot recently. (*Pause*)
  sr (b) Yes, I think you're right.
In the next four questions try to give both positive and negative tag endings to your comments on the following situations. Pause the tape after the word *either*, and say both versions aloud before you listen to the suggested responses.
7 If you think your radio is broken, you could say either . . . (*Pause*)
  It's not working, is it? *or* (*Pause*)
  It's broken, isn't it?
8 If you have not enjoyed a TV programme that has just finished, you could say either . . . (*Pause*)
  It wasn't very good, was it? *or* (*Pause*)
  That was terrible, wasn't it?
9 If you feel that the jacket you have just put on doesn't look right, you could say either . . . (*Pause*)
  This doesn't look right, does it? *or* (*Pause*)
  This looks wrong, doesn't it?
10 If you think that the politician you've just been listening to spoke badly, you could say either . . . (*Pause*)
  He spoke badly, didn't he? *or* (*Pause*)
  He didn't speak very well, did he?

Notes on the tapescript

1 Check high-fall on *wasn't it?* (b) is too formal, (c) even more so.
2 Check high-fall on *doesn't he?* (a) is non-connecting, (c) the same. *Oh yes*, provides the link.
3 Direct agreement is needed. (a) is inappropriate, (b) shows literal misunderstanding.
4 sr shows development of subject linked by, *Oh that reminds me,* . . . (b) has no link, (c) is possible, but the link is not clearly defined. This technique is used when changing the subject.
5 Qualified agreement is required, so (c). (a) is an inappropriate contradiction of the less important element in the utterance, (b) has

an equally inappropriate and offensive agreement with the less important element.

6 Affirmation is required, so (b). (a)'s question is just possible if the intention is to make the first speaker continue, which is unlikely here. (c) does not provide a connecting link.

7–10 In all the student responses, check for high-fall on question tags.

Exercise 4

Tapescript

1 You want to know if someone agrees with you that meat is very expensive nowadays. You say: (*Pause*)
SR Meat's very expensive nowadays, don't you agree?

2 Someone you know is talking about changing his job. You want to tell him that a mutual friend, Clarence, is also thinking of changing his job. You say: (*Pause*)
SR Oh, by the way, did you know that Clarence is thinking of changing his job, too?

3 You're not sure that your listeners understand the point you're making about the problems of living in a city. You end by saying, *It's all very difficult . . .*, and then what? (*Pause*)
SR It's all very difficult. Do you see what I mean?

4 Your boss is talking about next year's sales targets. You want to tell him that last month's sales figures were much higher than anyone expected. You say . . . (*Pause*)
SR Incidentally, our sales figures for last month were much higher than we expected.

5 You feel that you're not explaining yourself very well when talking about your home country to a group of foreigners. You end by saying, *It's all very different from England . . .* and then what? (*Pause*)
SR It's all very different from England – d'you know what I mean?

6 Someone is telling you about a Paul Newman film he saw on TV. You want to tell him that a new Paul Newman film is opening next week. You say . . . (*Pause*)
SR Talking of Paul Newman, there's a new film of his opening next week. Did you know?

Notes on the tapescript

1 *Do you know what I mean?* is an acceptable alternative in a longer discourse, but not here.

2 *Incidentally* is equally acceptable here to change the subject.

3 *Do you know what I mean?* is also acceptable.

4 *By the way* is a less formal register, and therefore not so appropriate in this business context.

5 SR practises the most common way of covering confusion and checking understanding.

6 sᴿ practises a variant form. *By the way* and *Incidentally* are just as effective here.

Exercise 5

Ask students to suggest variants on the phrases reviewed. Allow them to add acceptable variants to their books, unless they appear in Unit 5 of Section A or Section B.

Pairwork, groupwork and roleplay suggestions

Refer back to the students' written continuations of the phrases in Exercise 1 (supplementary exercise). In the light of subsequent practice (Exercises 2, 3, 4, 5), ask them to use these monitored sentences as the basis for conversation in pairs or groups, extending or developing their original ideas.

Unit 6 **Agreeing and disagreeing**

Checkpoint

Notes for guidance

1a They are probably discussing clothes that Betty is going to buy or wear.

  b Richard's off-hand agreements show he is not very interested in the subject.

Roleplay Students to enact and develop this situation in pairs, and then reverse roles.

2 Triple agreement here indicates lack of knowledge and/or interest in the subject under review.

3a Husband and wife discussing the delivery of Christmas presents.

  b Firm agreement phrases:
  Right.
  Weaker agreement phrases:
  Yeah, I suppose so.
  Well, yes.
  Firm disagreement phrases:
  . . . but don't forget that . . .
  Yes, but the point is . . .
  That's all very well, but . . .
  Oh come on . . .!
  Look, let's just leave it, shall we?
  Weaker disagreement phrase:
  Oh, I don't know . . .

4a Rick's point of view is somewhat overstated and an oversimplification.

  b Dave begins by using a very restrained disagreement phrase (perhaps ironically?), and becomes more firm in his disagreement as Rick seeks to enforce his point of view.

  c They agree to end the conversation <u>before</u> they get very angry.

  d Dave does not necessarily dislike the Michael Jackson record – this is another example of disagreeing with a specific, not total, concept.

Roleplay Students enact and develop the above situation in pairs as Rick and Dave.

5a George and Davina must know each other very well.

  b Their general casualness of language suggests that they are perhaps younger than Donald and Diana, but also perhaps a married couple.

c Agreeing phrases:
 Well, maybe.
 Yes, I suppose so . . .
 Well, yes . . .
 Yeah, OK.
 Disagreeing phrases:
 Oh, I don't know.
 Well, yes, but . . .
 Well, I wouldn't say that exactly.
 Oh, come off it!
 I can't go along with that.
 Oh, come on!
 Oh, leave it out!
 Look . . .
 I don't seem to be getting through to you at all.
d The conversation as a whole is highly unproductive in terms of shared agreement.
e It is not very important to either speaker (cf. the cassette recording).
f It provides an example of time-filling discussion between (married) couples, and was actually transcribed from a live situation.

Play the model exchanges on the cassette for the students to listen to, repeat and practise. Monitor for intonation, etc.

Exercise 1

Supplementary exercise   Get students to provide written continuations of each phrase and then practise saying them aloud. Monitor for tone, appropriateness and effect.

Exercise 2

Suggested answers are as in the tapescript for Exercise 3. Any deviant responses should be examined for differences in tone, appropriateness and effect.

Exercise 3

This is a slightly irregular exercise. Students hear five dialogues minus the key phrases, which they have to insert using those chosen in Exercise 2. Pause the recorder to allow them to do so. At the end of the five exchanges they will hear the suggested completed exchanges.

Tapescript

1 A I think it's better if we go on Thursday, don't you? (*Pause*)

   B ————.

   A Although it's easier to park if we go on Wednesday, isn't it? (*Pause*)

   B ————.

2 A Why don't we <u>rent</u> a video instead of buying one? It's much less expensive! (*Pause*)

   B ———— you have to keep on paying the rental charges for ever – and that's more expensive in the long run.

3 A If you ask me, all children do is reduce the freedom of their parents. (*Pause*)

   B ————. Children <u>do</u> give their parents a lot in return. (*Pause*)

   A ————, but they <u>demand</u> so much time, so much commitment! (*Pause*)

   B ———— when you have children you find that you give that time and commitment willingly, if you see what I mean. (*Pause*)

   A ————! I know lots of people who <u>don't</u> give it willingly – and who regret having children. (*Pause*)

   B ————; all I mean is that until you've <u>had</u> children you really can't predict how you're going to react. (*Pause*)

   A ————! I know exactly how I would react – badly! (*Pause*)

   B ————? Let's change the subject, shall we?

4 A If we ask Susan, we've got to ask Tony too. (*Pause*)

   B ———— – I think Susan would be very pleased to come without him for once. (*Pause*)

   A ————! She's lost without him, especially in public! (*Pause*)

   B ————? I thought she always argues with him when they're out together.

   A Yes, she does, but they both enjoy a good argument. (*Pause*)

   B ———— what about our other guests? They won't want to be involved in a family row, will they? (*Pause*)

   A ————. It would provide a bit of drama, wouldn't it?

5 A There's no point stopping your studies just when you're beginning to make progress, is there? (*Pause*)

   B ———— learning English is expensive, and I haven't got that much money! (*Pause*)

   A ———— You're not exactly poor, are you?

   B No, but I'm not made of money either. (*Pause*)

   A ———— you'll be throwing your money away if you stop now. (*Pause*)

   B ————! I'm very happy with my English now and I'm quite happy about stopping. (*Pause*)

   A ————! Don't you understand, if you stop now you'll have to go home. I shall never see you again and . . . (*Pause*)

   B ————!

You will now hear the five exchanges completed. Do they differ from the way you completed them?

1 A I think it's better if we go on Thursday, don't you?
 B Uh, huh.
 A Although it's easier to park if we go on Wednesday, isn't it?
 B Yeah, I suppose so.

2 A Why don't we rent a video instead of buying one? It's much less expensive!
 B Well, yes, but don't forget that you have to keep on paying the rental charges for ever – and that's more expensive in the long run.

3 A If you ask me, all children do is reduce the freedom of their parents.
 B Well, I wouldn't say that exactly. Children do give their parents a lot in return.
 A Well, maybe, but they demand so much time, so much commitment!
 B Yes, but the point is that when you have children you find that you give that time and commitment willingly – if you see what I mean.
 A No, I can't go along with that! I know lots of people who don't give it willingly – and who regret having children.
 B You really don't understand what I'm getting at; all I mean is that until you've had children you really can't predict how you're going to react.
 A Oh, come off it! I know exactly how I would react – badly!
 B There's no way we're going to agree on this, is there? Let's change the subject, shall we?

4 A If we ask Susan, we've got to ask Tony too.
 B Oh, I don't know – I think Susan would be very pleased to come without him for once.
 A You can't be serious! She's lost without him, especially in public!
 B You're joking, aren't you? I thought she always argues with him when they're out together.
 A Yes, she does, but they both enjoy a good argument.
 B That's all very well, but what about our other guests? They won't want to be involved in a family row, will they?
 A Well, I don't know! It would provide a bit of drama, wouldn't it?!

5 A There's no point stopping your studies just when you're beginning to make progress, is there?
 B You don't seem to realise that learning English is expensive, and I haven't got that much money!
 A Come off it! You're not exactly poor, are you?
 B No, but I'm not made of money either.
 A Yes, but the point is you'll be throwing your money away if you stop now.
 B No, no; you've got it all wrong! I'm very happy with my English now and I'm quite happy about stopping.
 A I don't seem to be getting through to you! Don't you understand, if you stop now you'll have to go home. I shall never see you again and . . .
 B Look, let's just leave it, shall we?

Notes on the tapescript

1 The first question demands simple agreement; the second less firm agreement. The third phrase offered, *No, I can't go along with that*, is too strong for the situation.
2 The other phrase offered is an over-emphatic rejection of the rest of the answer.
3 Gap one – qualified but firm disagreement.
  Gap two – grudging agreement.
  Gap three – disagreement in the form of introducing a new counter-argument.
  Gap four – stronger disagreement with this counter-argument.
  Gap five – disagreement by assuming the other person's misunderstanding of your viewpoint.
  Gap six – aggressive (sarcastic) disagreement.
  Gap seven – acceptance of the impossibility of reaching an agreement ends in termination of the discussion.
4 Gap one – mild disagreement.
  Gap two – surprised or critical disagreement.
  Gap three – as for gap two, but with the possibility of a genuine question.
  Gap four – directs disagreement to a specific area.
  Gap five – half-joking disagreement. Use of *Well* implies that A is seriously considering the possibility.
5 Gap one – disagreement which refers the other person to a fact or opinion overlooked.
  Gap two – surprised and critical disagreement. Quite aggressive in this context.
  Gap three – A then re-directs his argument at a specific point.
  Gap four – strong disagreement as A shows no signs of modifying his general line of argument.
  Gap five – A concedes lack of communication before going on to reveal his true reason for holding his opinion.
  Gap six – B then decides to terminate the discussion.
Ask students to analyse and discuss background and possible continuation of this exchange.

Exercise 4

Tapescript

1 Ten o'clock is better than eleven thirty, don't you think?
  Agree firmly. (*Pause*)
  sʀ Yeah, sure.
2 And it's very important that we don't come late.
  Agree strongly. (*Pause*)
  sʀ Oh, absolutely.

3 Oh I must buy that coat! Don't you think it's the most beautiful coat you've ever seen?
You're not sure – and it looks very expensive. (*Pause*)
sr Well, I wouldn't say that exactly. It's very nice, but there are . . .

4 So, we've got to have it ready by Thursday, whatever happens.
Point out that the machinery is broken. It's impossible. (*Pause*)
sr Yes, but the point is, the machinery is broken. We can't do it!

5 Caruso was the greatest singer there's ever been.
You think this is a ridiculous idea. (*Pause*)
sr You can't be serious!

6 So if you go with Brian, it will be better for everybody, won't it?
Agree reluctantly. (*Pause*)
sr Yeah, I suppose so.

7 . . . And so most foreigners are learning English because they really want to become more like English people.
Disagree totally. (*Pause*)
sr No, no, no, you've got it all wrong! People learn English to communicate . . .

8 Oh, I see! You think we should have the cheese before the main course and the dessert after the coffee!
This is exactly the opposite of what you've been explaining. (*Pause*)
sr I don't seem to be getting through to you. What I think is that we should have . . .

9 So you think that Gerald is really better off without Daphne, do you?
This is not the point you want to make: you think Gerald will learn to live without Daphne. (*Pause*)
sr You really don't understand what I'm getting at, do you? I simply feel that Daphne is not absolutely essential to Gerald . . .

10 No, I can't go along with that – you don't seem to realise that I've spent a lot of time thinking about this subject and I'm sure I'm right: marriage is a waste of time!
Try to end this discussion and move to a different topic. (*Pause*)
sr Look, let's just leave it, shall we? Have you seen Arthur recently? I hear . . .

Notes on tapescript

1 The prompt calls only for a simple short agreement.
2 sr revises *Absolutely* used on its own to show full agreement.
3 The situation demands tactful disagreement and the start of an explanation for disagreeing.
4 The prompt given as an order should provoke direct contradiction, with a short explanation of why the task is not possible.
5 The prompt calls for the contemptuous response given in the sr.
6 sr is an example of reluctant agreement. Correct firmer agreement phrases if these are offered.
7 An extreme and possibly offensive opinion provokes a total irate disagreement form. Check for raised pitch response against the cassette model.

8 Impatient disagreement is called for – hence the sarcasm chosen in the sr.
9 Here the first speaker has simply misunderstood (unlike the speaker in 8). Thus sr is less sarcastic, although still impatient!
10 The first speech makes it clear that the speaker is not going to change his viewpoint, and thus the student disagrees with it. The sr closes the discussion and moves to another topic.

Exercise 5

Ask students to suggest variants on the phrases reviewed. Allow them to add acceptable variants to their books, unless they appear in Unit 6 of Section A or Section B.

Pairwork, groupwork and roleplay suggestions

Refer back to the students' written continuations of the phrases in Exercise 1 (supplementary exercise). In the light of subsequent practice (Exercises 2, 3, 4, 5), ask them to use these monitored sentences as the basis for conversation in pairs or groups, extending or developing their original ideas.

Unit 7 **Getting what you want, making requests, giving and refusing permission**

Checkpoint

Notes for guidance

1a Although Enid adopts a mild form of refusal, her continuation makes it clear that she has not accepted the advice given.
  b Harry <u>is</u> concerned, hence his *really should*.
  c *Roleplay* Students should enact and develop the situation as the characters given, and then as themselves.

2a Persuading/advising phrases:
  I would be inclined to . . .
  . . . if I were you . . .
  I know it may be difficult, but . . .
  I really think you ought to . . .
  I'm sure . . .

  b Responses to persuasion:
  That's all very well, but . . .
  I just don't know if . . .
  . . . do you really think so?
  . . . it's very nice of you to say so – but I'm not really convinced.

  c The technique is flattery, . . . *your English is so good already . . .* etc., and Clara reacts by showing surprise and pleasure, *Oh, do you really think so?* – a perfectly natural response!
Roleplay Students enact and continue the exchange, with further persuasion and reaction.

3a Daphne is persuading Grace <u>not</u> to propose to her fiancé. Grace rejects her persuasion, so she will probably propose unless Daphne tries a bit harder.
  b *Roleplay* Students adapt, enact and develop this situation in pairs or groups.

4 and 5a The persuading techniques in 4 are intimate and personal, those in 5 more formal and elaborate.
  b 4 takes place in a shop, 5 in an office.
  c Sally and Brenda could be friends or workmates, or possibly daughter and mother.
  d Bruce and Neil's relationship is harder to pinpoint. Neil is perhaps a new manager trying to make some changes. Bruce is probably junior in position but senior in age and length of service with the company. Discuss students' analysis of these situations.

 e If Brenda is to buy the dress, Sally will now have to persuade her
 that she doesn't want her to buy it just so that she (Sally) can wear
 it.
Roleplay   Female students continue the discussion (4) on these lines.
 f Bruce expresses only grudging acceptance of Neil's persuasion.
Roleplay   Male students enact and continue situation 5, with further
reasons for Neil's contention and further reactions from Bruce. Of
course, if preferred, either roleplay can be enacted by either sex.

 6a Debbie has bumped into someone's – probably the boss's – car in
 the staff car park.
 b Arnold is clearly a junior manager – and one who sticks rigidly to
 the rules, enjoying the position of power he finds himself in.
 c Debbie is determined to persuade him not to tell on her, and, from
 his last speech, her persuasion is clearly working.
 d Other persuasion techniques she could use would be flattery,
 threats or temptation.
 e In the circumstances, Arnold will probably accede to her wishes.
Roleplay   Students enact and continue this exchange as Arnold and
Debbie.

Play the model exchanges on the cassette recorder for the students to
listen to, repeat and practise. Monitor for intonation, etc.

Exercise 1

Supplementary exercise   Get students to provide written continuations
of each phrase and then practise saying each one aloud. Monitor for
tone, appropriateness and effect.

Exercise 2

Suggested answers are as in the tapescript for Exercise 3. Any deviant
responses should be examined for differences in tone, appropriateness
and effect.

Exercise 3

Remember to pause the cassette recorder to give students time to
respond.

Tapescript (a)

1 Your friend is unsure where to go on holiday this year. Persuade him that
Malta is a splendid place for a holiday. (*Pause*)
 sʀ Have you thought of going to Malta? It's a fabulous place.

2 A relative coughs continuously. You know he smokes eighty cigarettes a day and has done for twenty years. Persuade him to cut down. (*Pause*)
sʀ I know it may seem difficult, but I really think you ought to cut down on the number of cigarettes you smoke.
3 Persuade your friend to buy a digital watch – it looks terrific, but he thinks it's too expensive. (*Pause*)
sʀ Oh go on, buy it, it's not that expensive!
4 Someone you know can't decide whether to buy a sports car or a hatchback. On balance you think he should get the hatchback. (*Pause*)
sʀ I would be inclined to get the hatchback if I were you.
5 You're rather annoyed with a colleague who always parks his car dangerously. Persuade him that this could cause an accident. (*Pause*)
sʀ Has it never occurred to you that someone could have an accident because your car's parked like that?
6 Your cousin doesn't know whether to see the dentist or not. He hasn't been for two years. Persuade him that it would be best for him to go. (*Pause*)
sʀ You really should go to the dentist, you know.

Notes on the tapescript

1 Fall-rise nucleus on *Malta* in the first sentence.
2 sʀ admits difficulty of accepting advice, and the reason for urging it.
3 A friendly situation provokes direct persuasion. Two tone groups – high-falls on *buy* and *that*.
4 Nucleus on *hatchback*; balanced tone needed throughout.
5 Monitor for staccato delivery of the advice in an annoyed mood. Compare with the cassette. Nucleus on *accident*. High-fall.
6 Nucleus on *should*, not *go* or *dentist*. High-fall with rise on *know*.

In the second part of this exercise you will hear the six pieces of advice from Exercise 2b. Reply as naturally as you can, and then compare your response with the one you hear.

Tapescript (b)

1 You really should buy a dog, you know. (*Pause*)
sʀ That's quite a good idea, but dogs are a lot of trouble to look after, aren't they?
2 Don't you think you should study a bit longer every day? (*Pause*)
sʀ That's easier said than done. I work very long hours already, you know.
3 I'd be inclined to buy the most expensive pair if I were you – they'll last much longer. (*Pause*)
sʀ You don't seem to realise that they cost four times as much as the cheaper ones!
4 It may be a bit difficult to organise, but you really ought to come and live in England for a few years. (*Pause*)
sʀ That's all very well, but I really don't think I could leave my family and my job for as long as that!

5 You must go and get a new suit – that one looks so shabby! (*Pause*)
  SR Mm, I suppose you're right, but I'm very fond of this old suit – I've had it for five years, you know.
6 Don't you think that, if you went to America, you'd learn to speak English much better? (*Pause*)
  SR I don't think that's very likely – it's quite a different type of English there, and I've studied British English for quite a time now!

Notes on the tapescript

This is a free exercise. The SRs have been chosen to illustrate a variety of possible responses. Admit any appropriate variants for the six provided. Check also for appropriateness of students' continuations.

Exercise 4

Tapescript

1 What should I do – go to the theatre or visit my sister in hospital? (*Pause*)
  SR Don't you think you should visit your sister?
2 But I visited her only last week – and the hospital is very depressing. (*Pause*)
  SR I still think you should go – she'd really appreciate it!
3 I have a horrible feeling that the boss is not happy about the report I wrote. He hasn't actually said anything, but I'm really rather worried about it. What do you think I should do? (*Pause*)
  SR I'd be inclined to ask him about it straight out if I were you.
4 Right, off we go, then – oh, do you want to do up your seat belt? Personally I never bother with them, but you can if you want. (*Pause*)
  SR You really should do yours up, you know. It's very dangerous not to – and it's illegal now, too.
5 I think I've left it too late to tell him: I'd really be too embarrassed to mention the subject now – and it's not that much he owes me. (*Pause*)
  SR Well, I know it may be embarrassing, but I really think you ought to tell him about it. He's probably just forgotten.
6 Shall I phone her? I've only met her once and she probably won't remember me. (*Pause*)
  SR Go on, phone her – she can only say no!
Now respond to these four pieces of advice or persuasion. Check your responses against those you hear.
7 Do you realise that if you stopped eating all those cakes you'd lose weight immediately? (*Pause*)
  SR Mm, I suppose you're right – but I love cakes!

8 Have you thought about the possibility of taking a degree course in English? (*Pause*)
  sr That's quite a good idea, but I don't think I'm good enough yet.
9 You know, they do say that too much exercise can be bad for you. (*Pause*)
  sr I'm not convinced by that – I think the more exercise you do, the better.
10 Has it never occurred to you that all this may just be a waste of time? (*Pause*)
  sr I don't think that's very likely. And, besides, I enjoy it.

Notes on the tapescript

1 The sr seeks to persuade by arousing a feeling of duty.
2 The sr reinforces persuasion. Monitor for use of *still*, *even so*, etc.
3 This is a difficult situation to advise in, hence the balanced advice. The sr adopts this with a limiting phrase, *if I were you*, as qualifier.
4 The sr rebukes as well as persuades. This is justifiable in the circumstances.
5 The sr urges the speaker to overcome his embarrassment and persuades him to a definite course of action, supported by a suggested reason for the third person's negligence. Students' variants should combine these elements.
6 This is a different type of embarrassing situation. The student's persuasion is based as much on curiosity in the outcome as in genuine concern for the speaker. A conspiratorial tone is needed, with the stress on *phone*.
7 The sr practises a form of reluctant agreement with the logic of the persuasion, but adds an emotional reason for not following it. A similar pattern should be present in students' variants, as complete agreement is unlikely in this situation.
8 The prompt offers a reasoned suggestion. A negative response should admit this before giving a reason for rejection.
9 The sr revises the rejection of a second-hand opinion used as advice, and then adds a counter-argument. Disallow student responses which refer to the opinion as if it were the speaker's, e.g. *I don't think you're right*.
10 The sr rejects the idea as unlikely and gives a reason for pursuing the current activity. Discuss and revise the uses of this form of refusal.

Exercise 5

Ask students to suggest variants on the phrases reviewed. Allow them to add acceptable variants to their books, unless they appear in Unit 7 of Section A or Section B.

Pairwork, groupwork and roleplay suggestions

Refer back to the students' written continuations of the phrases in Exercise 1 (supplementary exercise). In the light of subsequent practice (Exercises 2, 3, 4, 5), ask them to use these monitored sentences as the basis for conversation in pairs or groups, extending or developing their original ideas.

Unit 8 **Inviting, suggesting, accepting and refusing**

Checklist

Notes for guidance

1a Jim and Anne are obviously very good friends.
 b It is normal to check whether someone is free before suggesting a particular activity.
 c Anne is asking Jim to make a suggestion.
 d There are three forms: *Do you fancy going . . . ?*, *Let's go*, and *Why don't we go . . . ?*
Roleplay   This exchange can be continued. Having established the time and place of the film, there is the question of what to do before and afterwards.

2a Richard's suggestion is slightly more formal.
 b Richard is making his suggestion without first raising the question whether Betty is free that evening.
Roleplay   This exchange can be continued by suggesting alternatives and trying to come to an agreement.

3a Justin and Beatrice are not so close as Jim and Anne, and Beatrice does not want to make their relationship any closer.
 b Beatrice does not propose any alternative arrangements or actively encourage Justin to do so.
 c Invitations and suggestions:
   Shall we go out . . . ?
   I was wondering about trying . . .
   . . . What about Sunday?
   I was thinking of going to Brighton . . . is the first part of a more formal invitation.
 d His first approach to Beatrice was too casual and was turned down, so he now tries to be quite formal to see if that gets a better response.

Play the model exchanges on the cassette for students to listen to, repeat and practise. Monitor for intonation, etc.

Exercise 1

There are no particular intonation problems. Check for enough enthusiasm on such acceptances as, *Oh great!* and *What a great idea!*, and for a regretful tone on refusals, *Oh no, I can't* and *Oh, what a pity, I'm not free then.*
Supplementary exercise   Get students to provide written continuations of each phrase and then practise saying them aloud. Monitor for tone, appropriateness and effect.

Exercise 2

Suggested answers are as in the tapescript for Exercise 3. Any deviant responses should be examined for differences in tone, appropriateness and effect.

Exercise 3

Remember to pause the cassette recorder to give students time to respond.

Tapescript

1 I fancy having something different for dinner. (*Pause*)
  sʀ Why don't we go to a Japanese restaurant?
2 Shall we go to the theatre on Saturday? (*Pause*)
  sʀ Great! Where shall we go?
  Let's try to see *Cats*. (*Pause*)
  sʀ I've seen it already. What about *Starlight Express*?
3 What are you doing on Sunday? I'm thinking of going to the seaside. (*Pause*)
  sʀ Oh, what a pity I'm not free then.
4 What about this for an idea? Why don't we have dinner at my place and we can play your new record? (*Pause*)
  sʀ Love to!
5 Are you busy on Monday evening? I was wondering about trying that new Indian restaurant. (*Pause*)
  sʀ Oh no, I can't!
  What about Thursday, then? (*Pause*)
  sʀ I'm completely tied up all week, I'm afraid.
6 Gosh, it's hot! Do you feel like going swimming this afternoon? (*Pause*)
  sʀ What a great idea!

Notes on the tapescript

1 This is an implied request for a suggestion, so a suggestion must be made in response.
2 This is a two-part situation. sʀ1: react to the general suggestion and ask for a more specific suggestion; this is necessary for continuation of the stimulus. sʀ2 is lexically selected: non-acceptance plus a counter-suggestion. In sʀ1, high-fall nucleus on *Great!*
3 This needs a negative response; the available positive responses would be inappropriate in tone. An alternative response, *Oh no, I can't*, is not so appropriate in tone. Intonation: In *What a pity, I'm not free then*, nucleus is high-fall on *What*, with low tail.
4 This is a very informal suggestion/invitation, so a very informal response is needed. High-fall intonation.
5 A negative response is needed for continuation to sʀ2, which is lexically selected. *I'm afraid* should have a low-rise on *afraid* to sound

disappointed. If this was uttered as a low tail following a high-fall nucleus on *week*, the message conveyed would be that the person invited had no wish to go out with the other anyway.

6 This is a very relaxed invitation, encouraging a relaxed but enthusiastic response. Students' responses should convey this.

Exercise 4

Remember to pause the cassette recorder to give students time to respond.

Tapescript

1 You and a friend are trying to decide where to go on holiday. You would like to go to Tunisia. He says, *Where shall we go for our holiday this year?* (*Pause*)
   sr Shall we go to Tunisia?

2 He doesn't want to go there and says, *I'd rather go somewhere else. What about Crete?* You really like the idea. (*Pause*)
   sr What a great idea!

3 Your friend saw an accident happen, but the driver whose fault it was didn't stop. Your friend copied down the car's registration number. He really should tell the police what he saw. (*Pause*)
   sr Don't you think you ought to tell the police what you saw?

4 Your friend wants to redecorate his room, but can't decide how to do it. Suggest using wallpaper. It looks better than paint. (*Pause*)
   sr Why don't you use wallpaper? It looks better than paint.

5 You have just discovered that a film that you really want to see, *Gandhi*, is on at your local Odeon cinema. Invite your friend to come. (*Pause*)
   sr I've just discovered that *Gandhi* is on at the Odeon. Do you fancy coming to see it?

6 Your friends want to think of an interesting way to hold a party. You have just thought of an idea which excites you – hiring a boat on the river! Put your idea to them. (*Pause*)
   sr I've got a great idea! Why don't we hire a boat on the river?

7 Your friend cut his hand the other evening. It is very swollen and painful. Recommend that he goes to the doctor. (*Pause*)
   sr If I were you, I'd go to the doctor.

8 Your friend answers, *Well, I'll see. If it's not better by next week, I'll go then.* Recommend strongly that he should go this evening. It looks septic to you. (*Pause*)
   sr I really think you'd better go this evening. It looks septic to me.

Notes on the tapescript

1 The situation asks for a suggestion. The echo pattern used in the sr, *Where shall we . . . ?* followed by *Shall we . . . ?* is very common.

2 The situation invites an enthusiastic response. Students' variants should also show this.

3 The course of action is clear; a strong recommendation is necessary.

4 This is a straightforward suggestion for the other person to do something.
5 This is a relaxed invitation form, so a standard pattern is used: mention the event of interest and make the invitation.
6 The situation demands a really enthusiastic suggestion form, hence this sʀ.
7 This is a standard recommendation pattern.
8 The situation requires a strong recommendation. This one is appropriate because your friend is clearly not being very sensible.

Exercise 5

Ask students to suggest variants on the phrases reviewed. Allow them to add acceptable variants to their books, unless they appear in Unit 8 of Section A or Section B.

Pairwork, groupwork and roleplay suggestions

Refer back to the students' written continuations of the phrases in Exercise 1 (supplementary exercise). In the light of subsequent practice (Exercises 2, 3, 4, 5), ask them to use these monitored sentences as the basis for conversation in pairs or groups, extending or developing their original ideas.
Other more specific groupwork Deciding on the type of holiday and place to go; planning a party, etc.

Unit 9 **Approving and disapproving**

Checklist

Notes for guidance

1a Mr Johnson definitely does not have any towels.

 b *Seem* is used as an indirect softening form of complaint. (Compare its use when giving opinions, *It seems to me* . . . in Unit A5, B5, C5.)

 c He is talking to the hotel receptionist on the telephone.

 d Possible responses for last question:
 Have you looked in the wardrobe/cupboard/bathroom?
 I'll have some sent up immediately, sir.

Roleplay Students enact, develop and elaborate this and similar hotel complaining situations.

2a Simon uses *seems* for the same reason as in 1 – to soften his complaint and to allow him to leave with dignity if it is proved that the machine is working properly but that he has not been operating it correctly.

 b See the introduction to this unit in the Students' Book. The British attitude is to apologise for presenting the store (hotel or restaurant) with a problem, even though it was caused by them. This is because in practice this approach seems to get better and faster results (cf. Getting what you want, Unit A7).

 c The shop assistant shows reserved politeness.

 d He is not convinced – or does not want to be convinced – until he has looked at the machine.

 e It is most unlikely that he will give Simon a new machine without thoroughly checking the old one.

Roleplay Students enact and develop this situation as Simon (or Simone) and the shop assistant, who is first helpful, then unhelpful.

3a Suggested solution: they are in an open-air tennis court.

 b Gary and his friend have been playing tennis. Mr Tufnell is the caretaker who has been asked to stop the noise.

 c He himself is not bothered by the noise.

 d However, he has to stop them in his official capacity.

4 Complaining phrases (and half-phrases!):
 Look, Debbie, I'm sorry to have to say this, but . . .
 Oh no; not again!
 . . . you're always . . .
 Must you always . . .
 . . . why don't you . . .
 If you don't . . . I shall have to . . .

Will you please stop . . .

. . . what do you think you're doing . . .

Notice that Debbie uses 'familiar' complaining phrases, while Mrs Figgis uses more formal complaining phrases. This is because Debbie is younger and junior.

Roleplay   Female students enact this exchange. Monitor (with the other students) for intonation and development, and compare with the cassette model.

5a No. *Make* is used here in the sense of make or keep an appointment.

  b Kit is far more disappointed.

  c Carol's hesitation in her final speech suggests that she is not overkeen to rearrange her date with Kit.

  d Carol's hesitation also implies that her previous excuse could have been fabricated.

Roleplay   Students practise the telephoned cancelling of social engagements, with excuses and expressions of disappointment, and the desire to rearrange meetings.

6 This exchange shows stereotyped reactions to disappointment. The speakers either do not care deeply about George's failure or are unable to express their feelings with greater originality.

7a James uses formal, public expressions of disappointment suitable to the occasion.

  b His first utterance offers a conventional formula, but on receiving more information his second utterance demonstrates greater personal commitment, whilst his third is an attempt to cheer up Duncan – and himself – by stoic acceptance of the unavoidable.

Play the model exchanges on the cassette for students to listen to, repeat and practise. Monitor for intonation, etc.

Exercise 1

Supplementary exercise   Get students to provide written continuations of each phrase and then practise saying them aloud. Monitor for tone, appropriateness and effect.

Exercise 2

Suggested answers are as in the tapescript for Exercise 3. Any deviant responses should be examined for differences in tone, appropriateness and effect.

Exercise 3

Remember to pause the cassette recorder to give students time to respond.

Tapescript (a)

1 Ah, good morning. (*Pause*)
   SR I wonder if you could help me – I've got a bit of a problem here. I bought this calculator last week and it doesn't seem to be working properly.
2 Hello, reception? (*Pause*)
   SR There seems to be something wrong with the TV in my room. I can't get any colour.
3 Oh, Miss Evans. (*Pause*)
   SR I'm sorry to trouble you, but I can't get the new word processor to work properly.
4 Johnny! (*Pause*)
   SR Will you please stop jumping on the sofa like that!
5 Now then, Perkins. (*Pause*)
   SR I didn't want to bring this up, but this is the third time you've been late this week.
6 Darling! (*Pause*)
   SR Must you always leave your shoes in the middle of the room like that?

Notes on the tapescript

1 Note nucleus of the first phrase on *wonder*.
2 High-head on *seems*, not *wrong*. High-fall nucleus on T<u>V</u>.
3 Stresses fall on *sorry*, *can't*, *word* and *work*.
4 Monitor for the even stress and raised pitch needed in a strong complaint.
5 An admonishing complaint presumes the superiority of the speaker to the person addressed. Rising intonation pattern throughout SR.
6 This is a personal complaint: nucleus most likely on *always*.

Tapescript (b)

1 So it seems that Kiri Te Kanawa is not going to be able to attend the charity gala after all! (*Pause*)
   SR Oh no! How disappointing!
2 I'm sorry, I've got a cold – I can't make it this evening. (*Pause*)
   SR Oh no! What a shame!
3 Hello, Harry? Look, I'm really sorry, but I'm afraid I've got to cancel the dinner party. Audrey's got another headache and she's just not up to cooking for so many people . . . (*Pause*)
   SR Oh no! I was really looking forward to it.
4 Mum! I didn't pass! Oh, Mum! (*Pause*)
   SR Oh, well. Never mind.
5 Did you hear that Arthur didn't offer Terry that job after all? (*Pause*)
   SR Well, there's nothing we can do about it!

6 I've just been speaking to the director of Arpidec – they've decided <u>not</u> to invest in our firm after all! (*Pause*)

sr Oh no! That's a blow, isn't it?

Notes on the tapescript

The choice of responses is freer. Check against the intonation patterns suggested below.

1 This is a public expression of disappointment. Check for over-acting. Disallow a flat tone. The first phrase is fall-rise; the second phrase is high-fall.
2 Even if the disappointment is bogus, it must be acted convincingly, with rising patterns in both elements. *Oh* and *No!* are both high-falls; *What a shame!* has a fall on *What*.
3 As for 1.
4 These are consoling phrases, so a falling pattern on both elements is needed.
5 The slightly unusual consoling phrase requires the nucleus on *we*, not *do*.
6 Surprise and disappointment are expressed, so a falling pattern is needed in both elements.

Exercise 4

Tapescript

1 You bought a hair dryer from a shop and it only blows cold air. You are now in the shop where you bought it. You say . . . (*Pause*)
   sr Oh, good morning, I wonder if you could help me? There seems to be something wrong with this hair dryer . . .
2 You are really disappointed with the food in an expensive restaurant. How do you make this clear to the head waiter without creating a scene? (*Pause*)
   sr I'm sorry to have to say this, but that meal was not up to the standard I would have expected from this restaurant.
3 You are getting very fed up with a friend who always makes a peculiar clicking sound when he's concentrating. What do you say? (*Pause*)
   sr Must you always make that terrible clicking sound?
4 You are the chairperson of a discussion group, and one speaker is carrying on long after his allotted time. How do you make him stop? (*Pause*)
   sr I'm going to have to ask you to stop now – other people are waiting to speak.
5 You have lent your flat to a friend. You return to find a wild party going on. What do you say to your friend? (*Pause*)
   sr What on earth do you think you're doing?
6 Two of your subordinates at work have been seen arguing repeatedly in public and in front of fellow employees. You know this is bad for the company's public image. What do you say to them? (*Pause*)
   sr I'm sorry, but this arguing in public has got to stop – it's very bad for the company's image.

7 Two friends are getting divorced. What do you say to your wife or husband when he/she asks if there's anything you should do? (*Pause*)
sr Well, there's nothing we can do about it, I suppose – but it's very upsetting, isn't it?
8 A friend has cancelled an outing to see a film because of illness. You have already said you are sorry, now you want to fix another time. You say . . . (*Pause*)
sr Well, we must arrange another time to see it. Would some time next week be OK, do you think?
9 A famous film star was to have visited your club to give a talk. The club secretary comes in and announces that the film star is now unable to appear. You say . . . (*Pause*)
sr Oh no! What a letdown!

Notes on the tapescript

1 The sr revises public complaining phrases. Check for apologies and use of *seems*.
2 The situation requires coldly polite criticism. sr introduces the complaint with an apology and an indirect form of disapproval, here contrasting the meal served to the expected level of excellence.
3 This is a complaint to a friend, so it is far more direct. Variants, *Will you please stop?* and *Do you have to . . . ?* are equally acceptable.
4 sr expresses an obligation on the part of the speaker to complain, with a reason for so doing.
5 An angry response is required. Several variants are possible. sr presents one of the more self-controlled possibilities. Note the stresses on *earth* (low) and *doing?* (high).
6 A firm complaint is required whilst maintaining authority. Notice the impersonal form of rebuke: *It has got to stop*, not *I say you must stop it* or, *You must stop it*. This maintains the desired appearance of impartial authority.
7 This is included for the placement of nucleus on *can*. See Exercise B3, no. 5. Compare and discuss.
8 sr presents a common method of rearranging appointments. Students should analyse, repeat and practise in pairs at the end of the whole exercise.
9 This introduces the colloquial phrase *What a letdown!*, a variation of *How disappointing!* This is more for student reference than production.

Exercise 5

Ask students to suggest variants on the phrases reviewed. Allow them to add acceptable variants to their books, unless they appear in Unit 9 of Section A or Section B.

Pairwork, groupwork and roleplay suggestions

Refer back to the students' written continuations of the phrases in Exercise 1 (supplementary exercise). In the light of subsequent practice (Exercises 2, 3, 4, 5), ask them to use these monitored sentences as the basis for conversation in pairs or groups, extending or developing their original ideas.

Unit 10 **Apologising**

Checklist

Notes for guidance

1a Not really. Michael's use of *and all that* suggests that he is merely following social convention and nothing more.

b Yes. Michael wouldn't behave like this if he and Linda didn't know each other well.

c Linda is far from pleased; she is thoroughly annoyed.

d Yes, he does sound more apologetic.

e No, not sufficiently.

f Linda is being sarcastic.

g With very emphatic enunciation. With the lower part of the voice range, but the equivalent of high-head on *That's*, low-fall on *great*, and a pause between the two. Similarly for *That's absolutely marvellous!* low pre-head; high-head on *absolutely* and low-fall on *marvellous*, with pauses between the words.

h No, Linda doesn't want to be told! This is a standard sarcastic response to being let down.

i Michael is probably going to apologise very profusely; he will probably also make some unsuitable suggestion, like putting the food into the freezer until another day.

2a Simon is providing plenty of warning to Janet that he has done something pretty terrible – he is breaking it gently.

b He knows very well that it is not working at all.

c The use of *seem* in apologies is a standard formula; it is also used in complaints to remove any sense of aggression.

d Janet is being very sarcastic.

e Simon's apology is perfectly sincere.

f Low pre-head; high-head on *really*; fall plus rise nucleus on *am* and *sorry*.

3a Jim knows he is quite late.

b Anne is probably very annoyed.

c Low-head; low-rise nucleus on *usual*.

d *Par for the course* is a golfing expression meaning getting the ball in the hole in the number of shots a good player would be expected to take.

e Anne is using it sarcastically to point out that she expects Jim to be about as late as he is; he is doing well if he ever arrives earlier.

Play the model exchanges on the cassette for the students to listen to, repeat and practise. Monitor for intonation, etc.

Exercise 1

Intonation notes

Note the use of the upper part of the voice range for the apologies and confessions (so as not to sound sullen and surly), and the position of the nucleus on *am* in the sincere apologies. For the sarcasm, note the use of the lower part of the voice range and the very emphatic enunciation, with strong accents and pauses between words.
Supplementary exercise   Get students to provide written continuations of each phrase and then practise saying them aloud. Monitor for tone, appropriateness and effect.

Exercise 2

Suggested answers are as in the tapescript for Exercise 3. Any deviant responses should be examined for differences in tone, appropriateness and effect.

Exercise 3

Remember to pause the cassette recorder to give students time to respond.

Tapescript

1 Hello, have you still got my record by any chance? (*Pause*)
   SR I've got something I have to tell you. I'm afraid your record seems to have got scratched.
2 Ah, here you are at last. (*Pause*)
   SR Sorry I'm late. I got held up.
3 We're going round to the Italian restaurant for some lunch. Do you fancy joining us? (*Pause*)
   SR I'm sorry, I can't – I'm already going out.
4 Hello. Look, I'm sorry to be ringing so late, but I'm afraid I won't be able to give you a lift after all. (*Pause*)
   SR That's wonderful! Thank you so much!
5 Oh, so you're here, are you?! What sort of time do you call this? (*Pause*)
   SR I haven't done anything wrong, have I?
6 I don't want to sound pushy, but have you been able to mend that thing for me? (*Pause*)
   SR Sorry, I haven't done it for you yet. I've been very busy.
7 Hello, glad you've made it. We're still waiting for another couple to arrive before we can sit down to dinner. (*Pause*)
   SR I've got a bit of a confession to make . . . I'm afraid I've forgotten to bring that book with me.
8 Look, I'm afraid I didn't get anything for dinner. I simply forgot, I'm sorry to say. (*Pause*)
   SR Just brilliant! What are we supposed to do now?

Notes on the tapescript

1 This breaks the news gently and revises the use of *seem*.
2 You are only slightly late, so a very relaxed apology is all that's required. It follows the usual pattern – a brief apology and a brief explanation.
3 This is the only available refusal.
4 Heavy sarcasm is needed here. Your friend has really let you down. See no. 8 below.
5 This is trying to make light of it, like Jim. There could be many possible responses to this situation, but this response wouldn't fit any of the other situations in the exercise.
6 This is a simple apology plus an explanation; the choice is determined lexically by *haven't done it for you yet*.
7 Again, this is breaking the news gently.
8 Heavy sarcasm is used again. While the phrases in this and in no. 4 above could be reversed, the use of *we* makes this more relevant to the absence of dinner – for both speakers!

Exercise 4

Remember to pause the cassette recorder to give students time to respond.

Tapescript

1 A friend wants you to come round and help him with something next weekend. Unfortunately you can't, as you're going to be away. (*Pause*)
sr Sorry, I can't. I'm afraid I'm going to be away.
2 You are out with a friend. You were going to have dinner before the concert. You are waiting for your food. He has just told you he has left the concert tickets at home. (*Pause*)
sr That's just terrific! What are we supposed to do now?
3 Your friend lent you his camera. Unfortunately you left it in a taxi. How are you going to tell him? (*Pause*)
sr I don't quite know how to put this, but I'm afraid I seem to have lost your camera . . . that is, I left it in a taxi, actually.
4 You were supposed to meet your friend for lunch yesterday, but you just couldn't make it. Your friend is quite upset. (*Pause*)
sr I'm sorry about lunch yesterday. I really am. I'm afraid I just couldn't make it.
5 Your friend has just been telling you off for forgetting to phone to say that you wouldn't be home at the usual time. You don't think it's very important, as you are only a few minutes late anyway, and your friend always gets annoyed about little things. (*Pause*)
sr That bad, is it?

6 You promised to speak to your friend on the phone this morning, but his line was engaged. It is now afternoon and you are ringing him to explain. (*Pause*)
  sr Sorry I didn't speak to you this morning, but your line was engaged.
7 A friend was depending on your help with something urgent. You ring to say that you can't come to help after all. How are you going to say it? (*Pause*)
  sr There's something I must tell you. I'm afraid I won't be able to come and help you after all. I really am sorry.
8 The friend you were absolutely depending on to come and help you with something urgent has just rung to say he won't be coming after all. You're pretty annoyed. (*Pause*)
  sr That's just marvellous! What am I supposed to do now?!

Notes on the tapescript

1 This is a straightforward apology and refusal, with explanation.
2 This is a sarcastic response, revising the standard pattern.
3 The news is broken very gently. This is a really serious problem, so there is much hesitation. Any student variant response should show a similar lack of aggression.
4 A sincere apology is needed – your friend is upset.
5 This is making light of an excessive reaction by the friend.
6 This is not really your fault, so a straightforward apology plus explanation is all that is required.
7 Breaking it gently and being sincerely apologetic is essential – you are going to let your friend down.
8 Heavy sarcasm again. The matter is urgent and you were depending on him.

Exercise 5

Ask students to suggest variants on the phrases reviewed. Allow them to add acceptable variants to their books, unless they appear in Unit 10 of Section A or Section B.